PROMISES DELIVERED

PROMISES DELIVERED

A Sweet Werewolf Romance

TERRI S. STERN

Copyright © 2024 Terri Stern

All rights reserved. This book or any portion thereof may not be reproduced or used in any manner whatsoever without the express written permission of the publisher This book is a work of fiction. Names, characters, places, and incidents either are products of the author's imagination or are used fictitiously. Any resemblance to actual events or locales or persons, living or dead, is entirely coincidental.

This book is written in British English.

This book is intended for an adult audience and contains violence and profanity.

CONTENTS

CHAPTER 1

There was a delightful order to running a shop, even a ramshackle one such as 'Page Turner'. I'd been there five years, surrounded by books and papers and just a smattering of stationary to keep the regulars interested, and I was well attuned to the rhythms of the day.

The best shop at this end of the main shopping precinct, 'Page Turner' took up the full lower storey of the building with a very nice upstairs tenant occupying the upper floor - who made sure I got all the packages that showed up at irregular times. Mrs Wilson was a darling, even if she kept trying to set me up with her too young grandson.

Intermittently, I got new stock and took my enjoyment picking through the second-hand books handed in as they came to me. There were a few rare treasures, usually scooped up by one of the overly aggressive college tutors, but mostly I got books people did not love anymore, be it through their obsession passing or a relative doing the same.

It was not exactly a bustling town, Avon-on-Lee, but it was careful and regular, and people tried to get on with each other. It had been a good place to seek community when I was left alone after my mother's death, and while they still considered me unusual, I was welcomed in as part of the place once I'd lasted a couple of years.

This meant I knew, when the door opened ten minutes to closing, it was not one of my regulars walking into my shop. None of them would do that to me.

I looked up from counting the cash, bringing up my best customer service smile, only for it to die on my lips. Bastian Weir stood taking up all the space in my door, his broad shoulders blocking the view of anyone else accompanying him. It was unlikely he'd be alone - he wasn't often allowed to be unattended, given his position – but, as he closed the door and stepped closer, I noticed he had the decency to come in solo. Well, wonders never ceased.

He was as casual as I'd even seen him: dark jeans and a leather jacket that hung open to show a claret red shirt.

"Good evening," he said. His hair was neater than when we'd last seen each other too, the dark blond now trimmed into a business cut, even styled into some sense of order. It was all a little off, a little too unlike the usual formal presentation we had shared before, but there was clearly effort behind it. "It's good to see you again, Kat."

"Bastian." I nodded, going back to counting the cash. "We're only open until eight, so you're too late for browsing."

"My father died two weeks ago."

Shit. I stilled, looking up. He was grim faced but reserved, no tears or anger. Still lingering at my door. "I'm sorry to hear that. I know you were close. How's your mother doing?"

"The grief's hard. She's baring it well, but it's been a lot. She's staying with Marie just now."

"I'd have come to the funeral, if I knew."

"Thank you." His smile, while brief, seemed genuine. "His passing means I have to take over family matters."

"I imagine so." I glanced around my little shop, my heart sinking lower the longer the silence went on. "All of them?"

"Yes."

"Right." I swallowed, my responses evaporating in the desert between my throat and teeth. I had managed eleven years away from them. *Eleven.* It was stupid to think it would go on forever. But hope always died last, and I'd not heard from Bastian at all in the interim. It seemed like there was a good chance.

"I know it's been some time since we were promised." He stepped closer, peeking around the shop as he approached the counter.

"Years."

He nodded. "You've done well, setting up on your own. I know that's not easy with everything."

"Thank you." I tried to keep my tone level, with little success. My face heated, a flush to accompany the rush of words I trapped behind my teeth like a snarling dam, and I blinked back the furious tears that flashed behind my lashes. I would *not* have this conversation with him right now.

"My family could have made it easier."

"Not really." I closed the till too hard, the money inside uncounted and unbalanced, and turned away from his approaching form.

I retreated into the backroom, leaving him the shop as I got my coat and bag. He appeared at that door too, hovering just at it so not to crowd me into the space. "Kat—"

"Should I have told you to stay? Does that work?" I rounded on him, a hand on my hip and my coat tucked into the crook of my elbow.

He barked a laugh, sucking his lower lip in as he shook his head at me. "You weren't this rude at fifteen."

"My mother insisted on manners. I've had a while to unlearn them."

Bastian ducked his head. "I heard she'd passed."

"Yes. Five years ago."

"I'm sorry. It's a particular pain."

I stopped short, nodding as my rebuke died in my throat. "Yeah, it is. Same for you, I imagine."

"Different circumstances. Someone attacked my father."

"He was killed?" He winced at the question, but nodded. "Shit. That's incredibly stupid. Do you know who did it?"

"No, that's why I'm here. We're looking into matters, but until it's settled, you need to come to live with us."

"Pardon?" My bag slipped from my shoulder, landing on the floor with a loud thud. I didn't bend down to collect it, too focused on Bastian.

"We'll have to be wed, and quickly, given the approaching moon. You know that."

"But living with you? I have a life here."

He quirked his brows, tilting his head as he looked at me. "Did you expect us to be separate when married?"

"Yes! I don't even practice like my father. I'm no use to you. I thought you'd have found yourself some other wolf to tumble with and we'd be a technical marriage to fulfil your requirements."

He opened his mouth and closed it again, his tongue darting out to lick along his top lip when he dropped his head. His brows drew down in thought, I watched them make a dark little line of hair, before he looked up at me again, face tight. "Right. This will be quite uncomfortable then. I'm sorry. But I must insist that you come and live with me for the marriage, at least until my father's killer is found."

"What about my shop? Am I supposed to drop all of this?"

"For now, yes. Not forever, but it would be an obvious place for someone to target you."

"You're assuming they even know about me. Us. Whatever this is." I waved a hand between us, the gap, the distance I was keen to keep.

"The pack knows we were promised. My father kept track of where you were, that's how I found you."

My face flushed as red as my temper at that, the little barb almost enough to push me over the edge. "Oh, I recall." I spat the words, grabbing my bag up and pushing out of the door past him.

"What does that mean?" Bastian grabbed my elbow to slow me down, and I yanked my arm free, rounding on him.

"Don't play coy with me, dropping comments about making it easier. I remember how much my mother used to sob after your father came visiting, him or his friends."

He stepped away from me, hands up and palms facing me to show no harm. "I don't know what you're talking about."

"Spare me, Bastian. You're taking over the duties; I'm sure someone will fill you in on the proper etiquette for intimidation."

I stormed away from him, heading towards the door. He came up after me, keeping a few strides between us rather than grabbing for me again.

"I still need you to come with me, Kat," he said as I reached for the handle. "You're a potential target if someone's going for the pack. And I can't see any reason my father would be killed, if not that."

I clenched my fists as Bastian came closer, willing myself not to shout as I looked over my shoulder. "His line of work doesn't give you a few clues?"

"We're only enforcement, nothing that would necessitate a murder. Even if someone were angry about the nature of our work, it would be more obvious."

"There are usually tells, yes. Calling cards." I turned around to look at him again. He was so alien compared to the boy I'd known as a teen, dressed up smart to make a good impression. None of this felt right. I didn't know if it ever would. An arranged marriage when everyone who had arranged it was dead. Something about that seemed pitiful, and cruel, that we would be bound by the promises of the dead.

Bastian took a small step closer, smiling just a little. There wasn't much warmth to it, it didn't reach his already dark eyes, but he was being so careful. Even in my anger, I could see that. "I know this is sudden. I'm sorry. But I have to keep you safe, and the only way I can do that is by having you with us. For now. It doesn't have to be forever, and I don't want you to give up your whole life. I don't believe in that."

I swallowed, glancing at the door. No lurking body guards, no waiting heavies, just my little front porch. "Who's here with you?"

"I'm on my own."

I turned back to him, crossing my arms. "Bullshit. They never let you out on your own."

"They do now." He smirked, sliding his hands into his pockets. "It's been a while. I'm not on a leash anymore. At least not in the same way. There are some that can act as protection, of course, but I didn't think you'd like that for this news."

"So you drove up here on your own, hoping I'd be here. What if I'd been on holiday?"

"Then I'd have left you a note." Bastian pulled out a little notebook from his back pocket.

I laughed, then bit my lip despite it, rolling my eyes. "Charming. 'Time to get hitched, text me'?"

"I hadn't thought it through that far. I'm sure I would have come up with something." He stepped a little closer again. "Are you going to come back with me?"

"I don't know. Honestly, I don't want to." I sighed, looking around the shop again. "I need to think about this. And I want to know more about what's been happening. You weren't next in line for getting murdered when our families were friendly."

"It's been a while."

I shrugged, pulling my bag up by its strap. "My mother didn't want us tied in with it, after what happened."

"Your father was a good man. Loyal. It hurt my father, too, losing him."

"Loyal to a fault." I shook my head, unwilling to go back down that road. Taking a deep breath in, I settled my shoulders, chewing my lip before I spoke again. This was not becoming of me. While I might be alone now, I'd been taught manners growing up, and Bastian was grieving. The least I could do was be polite. "Come on, you can come back to my place. Have you eaten?"

He wrinkled his nose. "No."

"Fine, I'll cook for us both, then. And you can get me caught up."

"I can drive you over?" He pulled some keys out of his pocket, giving them a little shake.

"Sure. It's only a couple of miles, so I usually walk, but you'll be able to park easily enough."

"Yeah. I noticed there's not many cars around."

I sniffed, turning to leave. "It's a quiet town. I like that."

"Odd spot for a witch."

"I don't practice. Now shift, I need to lock up."

"Interesting choice of words," he said, smirk thick in his voice. Oh, he was going to be *insufferable.*

CHAPTER 2

Bastian followed me out of the shop, standing closer than I'd prefer as I locked up, like he was a lingering shadow. It was getting darker but not dark - the autumn evenings still light enough to see anyone else around, if that was his worry - and while it was chill, I hardly needed his body heat to stave it off. If anything, it made me over-warm, a flush of heat running up my spine. I turned back to him and he offered me his arm before he stepped back.

"No, thank you," I said.

"I have to be seen to be courting you, at least a little."

"Is that why you're here looking slick?" I tilted my chin at his jacket, the orderly hair.

He chuckled. "I'm not a teenager anymore, Kat. I try to take care with my appearance."

"Hrm." I wrinkled my nose. It was reasonable he wouldn't be the same as when we were teens. He'd have had his life with the pack just like my mother and I had made our own way. Eleven years. He'd probably gone and studied; his father had always been determined the children would have an education. "You'll have to tell me more about that."

"My appearance? You can see that for yourself." He smirked, pulling his jacket a little wide so I could see the red shirt underneath.

I rolled my eyes. "Ugh, you're worse than you were as a teen. Did you think that was smooth?"

"Smoother than I was then, at least." He gave a huffed little laugh, shaking his head at me. "Come on, it's getting chill out here."

He led me to the street, where a sleek black BMW sat waiting for us. It was clean, cleaner than I expected for him living out in the wilds, and while I wasn't easily swayed by cars, it was certainly not his father's hand-me-down.

"You like cars now?" I asked.

"I like a vehicle I know works. I'm all about something useful over something flashy."

"Nice." I nodded, laughing when he followed me round to open the door. "Courting?"

"Courting."

I slid into the seat, laughing to myself when Bastian closed the door and walked around. It was sweet, if a little old-fashioned.

"I can give you the address or just use my phone as a GPS?" I said, holding my phone up.

"I know your address." He turned the key in the ignition, pulling out smoothly into the empty street.

"That's not creepy at all, Bastian." I raised my brows at him. He kept his eyes on the road but his lips quirked in an almost smile, towing the line between bashful and a smirk.

"My father kept an eye on you after your mother died. That included knowing your address. Though I haven't been here before, so if there's a one-way system or the something let me know." He paused, chewing his lower lip for a beat. "Also, most people call me Seb now."

"Say again?"

"Instead of Bastian. You can be formal if you like, but the pack will call me Seb, so you're welcome to as well."

Seb? *Casual?* That sent my brain wheeling, totally unfamiliar to the formal structure we had as teens. I think if I'd called him anything but Bastian my father would have combusted. "Right. Noted."

"You haven't started to go by Kathryn now, have you?"

"No, still just Kat."

"Great, we can match then." He winked at me as we rolled up to a red light. "And at least we're good on names."

I rolled it over on my tongue, trying to match the sound up with him. "How long have you been going by Seb?" I asked as the light changed.

"A fair bit, actually. It was the name lots of the other wolves used, and it stuck."

"My father wouldn't have approved."

He snorted. "No, probably not. But he was a touch formal. All that ritual magic, I bet it instils a level of decorum."

"You could put it that way, yes. How's your sister doing?"

"Marie's fine. Enjoying having our mother with her, it's easing the grief a little."

"Can't be easy with it being an attack. Was it a wolf attack or a normal one?"

"Normal?"

"Human, I mean. There's a difference between having your neck torn out and someone shooting you." I regretted the words as I said it, too used to my own pain to pull the punch of the question.

"Ah." He laughed around the stutter, his tongue slipping out to wet his lip. "You mean, was it a fight?"

"Yes. Sorry."

"No, understandable with what happened. I shouldn't have left that unclear. They attacked him as a human, none of the usual signs of it being a rival."

I nodded, swallowed the lump in my throat as we drove along. "I don't know if that's better or not for you. For us, it would have been better."

"It means there are more suspects, but fewer difficulties between the packs. In theory."

"Oh?"

"Changes in the leadership are always fraught. It's not made any better when it's caused by a murder."

"No, I suppose not. I'm sorry." I put my hand on the back of Seb's, briefly, as he reached for the gearstick. "It's a hard loss anyway, and even worse when it's uncertain."

"Thanks." He smiled, and I pulled my hand back as we got closer to my house.

"It's just up ahead. You can park in the driveway, there's no one else uses it."

"No neighbours?"

"None that I rent my driveway to. The town's not big enough for that."

"Good, just didn't want to give you problems with anyone."

"Thanks." I smiled at him, wrinkling my nose at the easy pull he did into the driveway. Show off.

"Do you want a minute before I come in?"

"Are you assuming my house is messy?" I laughed, opening the door before he could answer.

"You weren't expecting company. Only seemed polite."

"Whatever you say. Do you need time before I come back with you, or is someone furiously cleaning while you're here?"

"I keep a cosy house, but it is clean. Largely." He held his arm out for me again and I shook my head, jogging up ahead of him to get up the steps first. Seb followed closed after, near in at my back while I unlocked the door.

"Are you following me like a shadow as part of wooing me?" I asked as we stepped into the hall. Our bodies obscured the dying light at the door, and I felt around for one of my lamps to click it on.

"I just want to cover your back. Until we know the cause of my dad's death, it's better to assume we could all be targets."

"That means you too, I take it?" I shed my jacket, hanging it on the coatrack I had tucked into the corner behind the door, and held my hand out for his.

"Yes. There's a suspicion I might be targeted as well."

"Who's covering your back, then?"

"Daniel's been with me most of the time."

"Little Daniel?"

Seb snorted, shaking his head as he handed the jacket off to me. "Don't call him that. You must have left before he had his growth spurt. He's taller than me now."

"Oh wow, he was such a lanky little boy when I was around. Of course he'd have grown, it's just…."

"You hadn't thought about it?" Seb leaned against the door to take his shoes off, a nice leather pair rather than hunting boots. He really had dressed up to see me. A pang ran through my chest, a little heavy tremor I shoved to one side.

"Not much. The shop takes up most of my time."

"And friends? Partners?"

"Um. Well. I haven't had much luck with boyfriends, honestly."

"Can't say I'm sad to hear it."

I scoffed at his comment, rolling my eyes as I walked away. "I'll have none of that yet, Seb. We haven't seen each other in a decade. I'm sure you've had some nice ladies to wag your tail, or however you would put it."

"Hey!"

"What? You were the pack leader's son. There were loads of girls with eyes for you." I clicked the lights on for the kitchen, turning to make sure he was coming after me. He wasn't, instead lingering in the open plan living room that was cluttered with books and my small TV. Maybe that could have done with a tidy, but it wasn't like it had any underwear left out drying or anything. That was the spare room upstairs. It was open plan through to the dining room, which abutted the kitchen and had a small door between the two to keep the cooking smell out, which gave me some cover to toss used cups into the sink somewhat subtly. "I lived there, I knew what went on, and—"

"Get here, now!" A shout rang through the kitchen, as a man burst through the door into the living room. He had a knife out in front of him, pointed at me as he charged closer, and I screamed without meaning to.

Seb rushed towards the noise, through the door at the same time the guy reached me, flinging himself at the moving shape, and I shoved my hands up in a defensive block as the knife swiped up towards me.

The man froze, then screamed, as his hands slid through the wall of fire that had enveloped me. Blue fire, magic; it itched over my hands, but it would never burn me. It was mine to use as I needed, and a blade coming at my chest was as good as reason as any. Shame burned more than the promise of the flames, at Seb seeing it after I had lied to him, and at my reliance on it rather than actually fighting. I could swing a punch if I really had to. But it was my family's gift. My father's gift, though it lurked in me too.

The man grabbed his arm; the knife clattering to the floor, before turning to rush past Seb and towards the front door.

I fell back against the counter, shaking, flames still dancing on my hands as I swallowed over and over, trying to cram the screams back down my throat.

"Kat, are you okay?" Seb stepped closer to me, hands up so I could see them. I blinked at him, brain still scrambling to work, and shook my head.

"You should go after him."

"Forget him, you're bleeding." He stepped closer, and I flinched away, tucking into the corner.

"Don't. It'll hurt you."

"No, it won't." He stepped closer, picking up a towel from the counter and starting the hot water tap running.

"What are you talking about?" I glared at him, trying to draw my fear back in to me, to settle it down so the fire would die back. It always leaped out worst when I was frightened.

"It's the same stuff your dad used to use, right?" he asked. He soaked the towel underneath the hot water, steam rising from the water.

"Yeah."

"He showed me it before. Before we were promised, even. It doesn't hurt me."

"That's impossible." I laughed, but it was a broken thing, short and too brittle in the enclosed space of the kitchen.

"Try me." He held his arm up. His forearm was thick, the muscles tensed, and a small fuzz of dark blonde hair reflected the flickering blue of my flames.

"What?"

"Grip my arm. Or just put a finger on it, if you're really scared. Your dad's fire didn't hurt me. I don't think yours will either."

"That's…" I couldn't find the words. Seb pushed his arm closer, just a little, and I gingerly put two fingers out to tap at the skin near his elbow, where the muscle was thickest and might not hurt. Nothing happened. The flames were there, slid along his skin like they did mine, but dropped away to the floor and disappeared like mist. "What?"

"Karl did it with me. It was a while before we were promised, maybe a few months. He showed me how it was safe so I wouldn't be scared of you. I think, he didn't really explain it."

I looked between his face and his arm, biting my lip. "Can I touch more?"

"Sure."

I grasped his arm, fingers slipping over the top of his forearm to grip the muscle closer to the elbow. He was fine. "This doesn't make sense."

"No?"

I shook my head. "The flames are to protect us, essentially. There's more to it than that, but in terms of anyone not within the family, they hurt. They didn't hurt my mother, because she was dad's love."

"It's always love." Seb said.

"Hm?" I let go of his arm as my flames died away, the hammering of my heart gradually lessening.

"It's always love, with magic. Love that binds things together, protects people from harm. Love keeps magic going even after someone has died. Shouldn't be a surprise."

"I suppose. He was devoted to us. Of course it would be love."

"Will you let me look at you now? You're bleeding and I want to be sure it's shallow."

I looked down and saw there was a line of red splaying across my blue jumper. The colours clashed. "It doesn't hurt."

"That's the adrenaline; it's going to. Take that off and I'll check it."

"Hell of a way to get me topless on the first date," I said. He frowned at me, wringing the cloth out. "Sorry."

"It's fine." He shook his head, brows down low as he turned and looked the other way. Sweet of him, I supposed.

CHAPTER 3

I stepped away from the counter to pull the material up over my head, hissing air through my teeth. Moving made it hurt, the burning sting rippling up my torso as I shed the layer, and I the skin was cold where blood already seeped out.

"That is a bit sore, now I'm aware of it." I set the top down, holding onto it with one hand as if letting go would cause something dreadful to occur.

Seb turned back, taking a deep breath as he looked at me. "That's to be expected. I'll get you some painkillers in a minute. Can I come closer?"

"Yes." I turned more towards him, grunting a little at the tug of the skin moving.

"Easy, Kat. Let me check you over. I'll need to wipe it clean." I nodded permission, setting my other hand on the counter so he had a clear view. At least I'd worn a nice bra today. It was such a stupid thought, it almost made me laugh. There was no way he'd care, and neither should I, but it would somehow be ridiculously worse if I've been in one of my washing day bralettes.

He ran the towel under the hot water again, wringing it out before he stepped up in front of me.

Seb's touch was feather light as he held me still, swiping at the wound with quick little semi-circles to clean the blood away. It stung every time the cloth ran across the cut, but it was a sharp little jab rather than the lingering pain underneath.

"I didn't know you were medically inclined," I said.

He glanced up at me, giving a lopsided smile. His lashes were dark enough that I could have counted them this close. "I'm not really. First aid certification and a few additional courses. It pays to be able to patch things up when a job goes sideways."

"Your pack had a magician on retainer and not a doctor?"

"We have a doctor, but you don't want to bother them for bumps and scrapes." Seb smiled properly, his grip tightening a little more. "This is going to need a proper clean and a dressing put on it. Where's your first aid box?"

"Under the sink." I pointed to the cupboard door.

"Great. I'm going to need you to lie down so I can do this properly. Can we do that on the couch?"

"Sure." He set the towel down and offered me his arm, which I took this time. Not that I couldn't walk - the shaking in my legs had stopped - and while my front hurt, the cut was shallow. Just bleeding a lot, like all shallow wounds did. But it was nice to lean into his side a little, as we went into the living room.

He tossed the throw cushions off the sofa except for one, which he offered me for my head. I took it for something to do with my hands rather than anything else, the arm of the sofa enough to prop my head up, and he gave my hand a little squeeze.

"You alright?"

"Not the happiest I've ever been, frankly."

He laughed, nodding. "Reasonable enough, beautiful. You stay still and I'm going to get the first aid kit. I'll clean the wound with an alcohol wipe, then do the dressing, and you can have some painkillers. That alright?"

"Sounds good." He left the room quickly, and I played with the throw cushion to distract myself from the bitter line of pain that ran from below my sternum to the mid-point of my chest. At least it had bumped over the joining strap of my bra. I think I would have died of sheer embarrassment if there'd been a nip slip on top of the rest.

Seb bustled back in, a glass of water in one hand and the kit in the other. "Can you lean up for me?"

"Sure." I propped myself up on one elbow, so I wasn't moving too much of my core, and he gave me a pair of chalky white, round tablets.

"Painkillers as promised."

"Thanks." I knocked them back, and he passed me the water, which I drank in small sips until about half the glass was gone. He took it away, setting it off to one side, and I lowered down, slipping my arm down the inside of the couch as there was nowhere else to put it.

"The alcohol wipe is going to burn, but then I'll dry it and put the dressing on, so just try to bear with me."

"I've had wounds before. Stop being so fussy."

"You're hurt. I'll be as fussy as I need to be." Seb knelt beside the couch, clicking the lid of the box open and taking out the pieces he needed. "We should speak about something else, too."

"Should we?" I didn't look at him, eyes fixed on the ceiling above. The house still had moulded ceilings; I had said I would change that when I moved in. At some point, I'd got fond of them, hideous as they were. Terrible for cleaning as well. They had character, though, one of the quirks of the place. May as well have some quirks when I was living there.

"Yes. You said you weren't practicing magic."

"I'm not."

"Kat." He shot me a look. "You can be cautious all you like, but don't lie to me."

"You didn't see anything. If you want me to come and stay with you, which I'll have to given what's happened, then you did not see that."

"What did I see then?" Seb took the little folded piece of cotton out, setting a hand on the arch of my ribs as he quickly wiped the length of the cut.

I hissed air again, the burn of the alcohol different from the cleaning. This was like being cut once more, blooming quick and cold across the wound, and I bit into my lip before I answered him. "The guy swung at me and I hit him with my bag. That knocked his hand into the stove, which was on because I was cooking for you. Us. And that caught on his clothes. That's how he wound up on fire."

"Very impressive." Seb discarded the wipe into the lid of the box, taking a clean cotton pad and drying the wound. He plucked up a dressing in its wrapper, judging it against the cut before he took a second one for the upper part as well. "I'm glad I have a wife with such good reflexes to pull that off."

"Had to be a reason they promised me to you. Quick reflexes are as good as any."

He hummed, taking the first dressing out and placing on my skin before fixing it with micropore tape. "I think there were other reasons, but it is as good as some indeed."

"Thank you."

"You alright there, Kat?" He set the second dressing on the skin at my chest, measuring small strips to fix it carefully outside of my bra. "Almost sounded like you were thanking me."

"You've done me a kindness. Only seems right to be polite."

"We can be more than polite, no?" He winked at me before he pecked a light kiss to the edge of the tape.

I batted the top of his head, rolling my eyes at him. "Easy, stud muffin. You might make me faint."

"You're already on a couch. It's the right place for you if you do."

I chuckled, pushing him away. "Is that supposed to make me feel better?"

"I thought it might raise a laugh." He sat back on his heels, scooping up the rubbish from the box lid. "This is a good kit you have."

"Thanks. It's sensible to keep it well stocked when you live alone."

Seb clicked the lid closed, standing up. "I'll take notes for the one back at the main house. Will you come tonight? With me, I mean."

I wrinkled my nose, but nodded. "If they already know where I live, that seems sensible, too. Not that I want to stay for long, but we're not safe apart, evidently."

"And the marriage? We'll be expected to wed shortly."

I sat up, tugging one of my stash of blankets around me. It was as much for modesty as for the chill creeping up my back. "I'll do the ceremony, for the sake of the pack. But I don't want to be some housebound mate. I'll leave once this… situation is resolved."

"Right." He nodded, then turned on his heel to go back to the kitchen. "If you want to go upstairs and pack, let me sweep it first. I expect they'd have made a move by now but the other one waited so better to be safe."

"Sure. We can go up together."

"Good plan. You might want to hit one of them with your bag again," he called. I brought my hands out of the blanket, turning them over to check for any marks from the fire. It would never burn me, but magic could do other things. I was fine, though. Better, for him having patched me up.

"Are you ready?" Seb appeared at the door again, nodding his head back towards the stairs.

I looked over at him, stood in another of my doorways. He was relaxed, even with a potential threat, filling up the space with his crossed arms and careful look. Better him than another knife, I supposed. "Sure."

CHAPTER 4

The rest of the house had been clear, no more lurking men with knives to stop me packing what I could fit in a suitcase and a couple of holdalls. It was sad to reduce my life to just that, but there were no pets to leave food out for and no partner to leave a note for, so it worked. And I would come back in a while, so it wasn't like I needed to take everything. I kept telling myself that.

I took my jewellery - I'd need some for the ceremony - and enough clothes, makeup, and books that I could probably beat any future attackers away if they popped up on the way from the house. Good luck running after one of those bags hit you. Seb had carried them to the car for me like we were going away, all easy smiles and not letting me lift anything. Courting, of course.

We were driving out towards Seb's home, into the dying twilight and through the long line of trees that flanked the roads like old sentinels watching us leave the town. I watched them back, eyes on the blur of green that flitted past, the shadows leaping between heavy branches as if something ran beside us.

"We should stop for food before we arrive," he said.

I turned my head back into the interior of the car, brain still a little frazzled from earlier. "Say again?"

"We should get you some food. And me, I suppose. Food's always better with company."

"You said you hadn't eaten." I played with my own hands, stretching my legs out in the footwell to point and flex my toes. It hurt the wound at my front, but I pushed the sting away; focused instead on the feeling of my thumb rubbing over my knuckles. "You should have had something before you came. It's a long drive."

"I was too nervous." He sat so easily in the driver's seat, like he was used to it. None of the tense focus of some people in the town, or the angry simmer of the road ragers with their shoulders up around their ears. I wondered again what he had been up to while we were separate.

"Why?"

"I didn't know how you'd take the news. It's hardly romantic, showing up and telling you about murder. Spilling grief all over."

"I'm well versed in grief. You don't have to worry about that." I patted his hand on the wheel, briefly. "It's not a problem to feel your feelings, Bastian. Seb." I wrinkled my nose. Still not used to that.

"I know. It's not something we're ashamed of in the pack. But it's not a nice proposal for you, either."

I snorted, covering my mouth with the back of my hand. "You never proposed to me, we were promised. You got to skip all that planning."

"Would you prefer I'd brought you a ring?"

"I mean, if it was that or a man attacking me in the kitchen, I would have taken the ring, yes. But it's unnecessary. I've bought my own jewellery, have done since my dad passed. And it's not like I'm your first choice. I'm practical about that."

"Don't say it like that." Seb frowned over at me, shaking his head. "I was always proud that we were promised."

"Really?" I twisted in the seat, regretted it at the tug of my scabbing wounds. There was no telltale popping of the tape though, he'd secured that well so I would have to be careful with it.

"Why wouldn't I be?"

"Because you're the son of the pack leader, you could have all sorts of potential spouses. Wolves, especially. I'm not someone that can run under the moon with you, or roll around with the pack. You could have your choice of nice… pelts? No, that sounds grim. Tails? Women who are more like you." I waved my hand to cover all the bases.

Seb snickered at my attempt to explain, a crooked smile tugging at his lips. "Witches are tied to the moon, too, no? Your father was."

"He was, he loved the moonlight. He'd read *The Highwayman* to me sometimes, when he was putting me to bed, or quote the lines while we were out walking."

"So you're not too far off, with the moon. I bet you can still quote the poem."

It brought up a fond smiled, and a soft comfort nestling in my chest, at the thought of my father's words. "You're right, I can. I can't change into a wolf, however."

"I don't know. You do pretty well with claws."

"I suppose that's nicer than saying I'm bitchy."

"I would never." He glanced my way, his smile close to my own. "The pack doesn't need you to be a wolf. It needs you to be you."

"The pack hasn't seen me in eleven years. They probably don't even remember me."

"They do. Marie gave me hell for not coming and getting you sooner. She can't wait to see you again."

"Really?"

"Sure as anything." Seb nodded, clicking the indicator to pull us off into a service station. "My mother was similar, though I think she had a bit more tolerance for my delay. She would have had me bringing roses and a champagne bottle, too."

"That's…"

"Old fashioned?"

"Not fair to you," I said, shaking my head to myself. "You're grieving. You shouldn't have to do performative rubbish like that when you're not long bereft. I was always going to be coming back with you."

"What on earth does that mean, Kat?" He turned the key to kill the engine, and the car was suddenly very quiet.

I swallowed, looking around the carpark rather than at him. "We're promised. It's not like I have much of a choice. Or like either of us does. No need to pretty it up more than that, there's an inevitability in all of this. I kept my shop, and you had your free years, and now we have to do what's expected of us until things are safer. It must be hard for you, too." I tried to give him a smile, but it was a half-formed thing, no genuine mirth in it.

He set his hand on top of mine, his broad thumb rubbing over the peaks of knuckles. "The idea of marrying you was never a hard one for me. I trust you to be as good a person as your father was."

"I'm not willing to die for the pack." I looked at him, lower lip bitten between my teeth. "Don't ask me to say I am because I'll not be able to lie about that. I saw what happened with my father and I'm not the same as him."

"No one was sure what happened with your father."

"My mother was." I crossed my arms, trying to pull my temper back in like an unruly cloud. His hand lingered on my thigh, shifting so the back of his hand was against it. Very gentlemanly.

"I know there were theories." He was being so gentle and I suddenly hated him for it, for treating me differently when it came to old pain. I was fifteen again, being told they'd already made all the decisions for me and I should be pleased.

I clicked my tongue to dispel the pain in my throat. "Don't, Bastian. We could do not to have a fight before we even get back to your house. I know your father defended the pack, and I know my mother left because she didn't feel safe after they found her husband with his neck ripped out. We don't need to say any more."

Seb's brows drew down again before he cleared his throat. "I don't want you to feel unsafe with us, is all."

"Unsafe like being attacked in my home? We're good on that. I would rather be with you than someone killing me in my kitchen."

He tilted his head to one side, then gave a little shrug. "It's a low bar, but we've passed it. Good start. Come on, we can get something here before we drive the rest of the way out."

He gave my thigh a little squeeze and opened his door, sliding out to open the door for me too. The air here was cooler, the chill of night stealing the warmth that had built up between us in the car. I shivered, a little, as I got out - the replacement top I'd pulled on was not as thick as my ruined jumper. I should have brought a jacket other than the coat I had slung into the case.

"Here." He leaned into the car and grabbed his jacket. "You can wear this until we get inside."

"Thanks. Won't you be cold though?"

He shrugged. "I run warm. Always have. Anyway, I kind of like the idea of it smelling of you. That's a cute couple's thing."

I nodded, sliding the soft leather on. It was well worn in, scuffed up at the wrists, and smelled of dirt and whatever cologne he wore, something clean and crisp. I took a deep breath as I pulled the collar closer, then realised what I was doing. "I like what you wear, scent wise. Suits you."

"Thank you." Seb gave me his arm, and I took it, for the sake of hiding my embarrassment at this point. There was a smattering of other cars in the services, but not too many, just enough that there should be chatter and bustle once we got inside. We could almost look like any other couple stopping for a meal together, and it was easy to slip into that sort of role as we got closer to the large glass windows shining away in the encroaching dark.

CHAPTER 5

The restaurant was the usual services affair: bright and breezy décor with a menu full of meat and carbs. Burgers and a wide variety of forms of potato, tortillas with all the toppings you could wish for, stroganoff and curry with enough rice to barter your way into some places. We were seated opposite each other in a cosy booth, perfect for couples as the friendly waitress said, and Bastian ordered us both soft drinks as we checked the menu over.

"I want to keep a clear head while I drive," he said as the waitress disappeared.

I smiled, glancing up at him. "That's no problem. I prefer you do. I hate people who drive drunk."

"I would have asked if you wanted a wine if you hadn't already had painkillers."

I laughed at the thin press of his lips, how he glanced to the open-sided bar, then back at me. "I'm able to order myself a glass of wine if I'd wanted one. As it happens, I don't. You're so fussy."

"They attacked you in your home, while I was there, beautiful. Let me have this one."

"That's the second time you've called me that." Our drinks arrived, and we ordered before I continued. "Is there a reason?"

"For calling you beautiful? You are. And I want to have some terms of endearment for you. I can't be calling you Kat all the time. It sounds stuffy."

"Does that mean I get to do the same?" I poked the ice and slice of lemon in my glass with the paper straw, enjoying the way they tinkled against each other.

There was a grin in his voice when Seb replied, just on the edge of teasing. "That depends, what did you have in mind?"

"I don't know. Fido? Spot? Spot's good, better than Clifford or Lassie."

He took a long sip of his drink before he put it down. "Not darling? Love? Sweetness? Honey?"

"All a bit overfamiliar, are they not?" I took a drink through my straw, batting my lashes innocently at him.

He wasn't buying it for a second, shaking his head at me as he set his glass down. "Kat, we are literally getting married."

"We are, and you only compliment me for my looks. Hardly the sign of a devoted fiancé. What else do you allegedly like about me? We should make some stuff up for the vows." I propped my elbow on the table, planting my chin on the back of my hand, and stared at him, brows raised.

"You're making it sound like this is a visa arrangement or something."

"No, but maybe we should take a lead from that, prep like they might ask us questions. You probably can't remember much about me from when I was a kid, and clearly all my memories are out of date, so we can trade updates on the drive up. We'll need to have some idea of things that make us wildly in love if we're going to sell this. Same way you're 'courting' me."

"I'd court you properly if it ended this discussion."

I winked, turning the gesture back on him, and he had the decency to look bemused. "No such luck, sorry, buddy."

"Spot was better." Seb took another drink and frowned at the glass like he wished it contained more than lemonade.

"Spot it is. I can say it's like sweet spot, but you'll know the truth." I sat up, the slouch of earlier making my tugging skin at my sternum hurt. "I like that you're first aid trained. Shows you're happy to care for others."

He blinked at me, almost laughing. "What?"

"I like that you went and did that. It had to be before your dad died, yeah?" He nodded. "So it wasn't you brushing up for taking on his role, you did it to help the folk you work with. That's nice."

"I suppose so. Well, if we're going at it from that angle, I like your bookshop. It has a nice variety of items, and you've kept it going a past the usual three-year point of peril, so you must take a lot of care with it."

"Thank you." I smiled at him, tilting my head to one side as I looked him over. "I like that you take care in your driving too, you're a skilful driver."

"Why do you sound so surprised at that?"

"Were you ever in a car with your dad? John drove everything like he stole it."

Seb snorted into his drink, wiping his chin with one hand when he pulled it away. "Do not say that in front of my mother. You're right, but she used to say the same thing."

"My lips are sealed." I ran a thumb and forefinger over them, as if to zip them closed. "Promise."

"I like that you've made your own way, not just with the shop. Your house is a friendly space. Homey. That's difficult to do when you live alone."

"I'm certain I should take offence at that, but I won't."

Our food arrived, interrupting his response, and once the waitress left, we were back on the precipice of almost feeling friendly. Almost. We looked at our plates, then at each other, before we started to eat.

"Did you ever think about coming to see me? Before you had to," I asked. I stole an onion ring off his burger while he formulated an answer, biting down on the too-hot batter but chewing, anyway. May as well commit to it.

"Yes." His smile was different this time, softer, as he took his napkin and laid it over his thighs. "When I finished studying, I wanted to come find you and tell you what I'd done. I was the first of the family to do it straight out of school, and I was all hyped up on that like it was something to brag about."

"That's awesome. I would've been happy to see you then."

"I found out about your mother passing before I would have come to see you. It would have seemed… insensitive to show up bragging about it when you were dealing with grief. I didn't know how to match that difference in the feelings."

"Whereas this time you did."

"Yeah." Seb stilled, eyes flicking over my face, and then reached across the table to grip my hand. "I've felt guilty about that since my father died. I should have come anyway, even if it was messy, and I didn't. That was badly done."

"Grief's a big thing. It can be very intimidating when you're on the other side of it. And I wasn't exactly nice to your father and Victor when they came visiting."

"What?"

"Did you never talk to your dad about me or something?" I pulled my hand back, picking up my burger to take a bite. It was petty to throw that at him, but he simply shook his head as he picked up his own bun.

"I didn't, much, honestly. He never raised us getting married, except after I'd finished my studies, so I let the matter lie. When did they come to see you?"

"Hm." I was too tired to decide if I believed him. "After she passed, the pair of them came to visit. They brought one of your mother's lasagnes, that was appreciated, and offered to pay for the funeral."

Seb frowned, setting his burger down. "They offered you what?"

"They sat in the apartment we were renting and offered to pay for the full thing, casket, ceremony, and the grave plot. It's expensive to die, you know. Well, you'll have found that already, sorry. But yes, they came and sat on the hideous little sofa we had there, took up all the space between them. Drank the cheap coffee I had in the cupboard and offered me a lot of money."

"And you said no."

"I think I actually threatened to throw a cup of coffee in Victor's face if he showed up at the funeral." There was a sudden heat around *my* face as I bit my lip around a shameful laugh. I had not been graceful, in the dark days after my mother died, I had been sharp and brittle as untempered glass. "It wasn't long after she'd went and I was still very raw. He was always pushier than your dad."

"Victor's a good man, but yes. Forceful. He's still involved with the pack, so you know."

I nodded, waving a hand as I went for another bite of the burger. "Of course, I presumed so. When I see him, I'll apologise."

"I'm sure he won't hold it against you, you were young and hurting. Why did you say no?"

"I didn't want to owe the pack anything. I was already tied in when the inevitable came around, but I wanted to do that for her myself. There were insurance policies to pay for the funeral, and I was going to have to make my own way anyway, so it seemed like cheating, somehow, to take it. Like I would be ignoring her wishes."

"You didn't have to do it all yourself."

"What else would I have done at twenty-one, all alone in the world? My dad's family has had nothing to do with us since he died, and there was no other family on my mother's side."

"You could have come back to us." Seb said it so plainly, like it was obvious and I was a fool for not seeing it.

"The pack?" I nearly dropped my burger, swallowing around nothing before I spoke again. My brain snagged on the idea, the option nestling in my head like it had laid itself out across the table before us. "It honestly didn't occur to me. I never expected to be coming back other than to fulfil our promise, and even then, I thought it would be for show. That you would have someone else who was your proper partner."

"We would have had you back in a heartbeat. You're not some enemy incomer, Kat, you were one of us until you left."

I looked down at my plate, mulling over my response. I didn't want to be cruel to him unnecessarily, but his reading of the situation was so far from mine I felt dizzy with the distance. "That wasn't how it seemed speaking to your father and Victor. It seemed very much that they were burdened by my being alone, and returning would have been the minimum expected to make up for my mother's indiscretion. For her wanting to be safe."

"Safe?"

"Well, much as she died, neither of us got our throats torn out in the dark woods. I don't know if we could say the same thing if we stayed."

"Kat, none of us would have hurt you."

I set my fork down too hard; the metal clinking against the plate like an angry note. "Someone killed my father. I know your lot swore down to the ground it wasn't one of the pack, but even if not, he was supposed to be protected. Instead, he was dead under the *precious* moonlight. And we were alone."

Seb made a pained sound. "You didn't have to be alone. I didn't want you to be alone. You were so walled off after it happened."

"I wonder why." I bit into the burger to stop myself saying something else cruel, old venom seeping between my teeth. We shouldn't talk about this, I'd said as much in the car.

"I know. Sorry." He picked up his drink, swirling the fluid inside for a few moments as he considered the bubbles spinning and tumbling. "I didn't know they made that offer. None of us attended the funeral, but I was told that was because matters had already been taken care of."

"They were."

"Yes, I see that. That's not how it was presented, but I see what you mean. I think I know what they intended in their offer, but evidently it was not communicated well." He sighed, setting his glass down as he tried to catch my gaze. "I'm sorry for that. I would've loved to be in touch with you sooner if that were an option."

"Thank you. I might have wondered about you a few times too."

"Yeah?"

"Just what you were doing. If you were off sowing your oats, or travelling. I didn't think you'd be allowed too far off being the golden boy. They never let you be on your own much when we were little. But maybe you'd get to do some different things. Road trips and whatever."

"Sounds like you like the sound of that." Seb started eating his burger again, watching me as he chewed.

"I'd love to travel. I used to have this plan laid out of where I'd want to go, backpacking so I could stay in places off the map. Get to explore cities for a few days at a time, maybe work on farms for like orange picking or whatever else I could find, live somewhere a while before you move on."

"That's not the safest way to do things, you know?"

"I know." I shook my head at him, pushing at the side salad I had. The cherry tomatoes were fine, but the greens were limp, evidently seeing the worst of the fridge at this late hour. I pierced a tomato onto my fork and wrapped some lettuce around it like it was a secret. "I thought it would be a good way to see the world."

"You didn't go though?"

I shook my head. "No. After my mother had her first stroke she needed help during the day, and that costs money. It was more important that we could pay for that than I got to go off gallivanting. I worked in the day and did classes at night, aiming for something better. Anyway, lots of time to do that in the future. It's not like only teenagers go travelling."

He hummed, finishing his burger. "It was good of you to see to her care."

"It's what we do, no? Marie's doing the same with your mother and her grief. You're here bringing me back to the pack so the necessary things can be done. We all try to care for the folk we love."

"We do, you're right." He tilted his head the other way, like he was evaluating something, then coughed before he spoke again. "Were you with her when she passed?"

I let out a shaky sigh, the leap of my heart in my chest a familiar but unwelcome pain. "I was at home, yeah. It meant I got to sit with the body until the funeral home could collect her. There's something grounding in that, getting to see that the person isn't there anymore. That they're gone. It's difficult, but helps you make your peace."

"Oh, Kat." He was out of his seat, scooting into the space beside me to wrap an arm around my shoulders. "Baby girl, I am so sorry."

"That's a new one," I said, huffing a little breath as I tried not to cry. It was all old pain, I'd had tears enough when she died, but it was suddenly pressing at me with all the talk of before. Crying in public was absolutely not what I wanted to do, though, and even with the privacy of a booth, it would cause a scene. I took a deep breath, settling my shoulders.

"I'll call you whatever you like, or I can keep rotating them, whatever makes you smile. Come here." He tugged me closer, running his free hand up and down my arm. "You were so brave doing that. I don't know if I could have done that then. I could barely do it now."

"You had to?"

He coughed, hugging me tighter for a moment before he spoke. "I found him. Well, his body. He'd been missing, didn't come back after a meeting, and I'm the best nose. Of course I went out to look."

"I remember that, about you being the best for finding a scent. I'm sorry, Seb, that's awful."

"It was, but at least it was me and not anyone else. Marie wouldn't have been able to handle it, seeing him like that. Better it was after they cleaned him up."

"Yeah, it makes it easier," I said. I held his hand, still on my arm, threading our fingers together to give them a little squeeze. It wasn't much comfort, but his pain was so much newer than mine. He deserved some softness.

He exhaled, resting his head against my shoulder. It felt warm even through my top, his skin radiating along the curve of the joint, lingering. "I keep running into old pain with you, darling. I'm going to have to make myself a map."

"Eleven years makes a long gap. Natural you'll have a few traps to fall into. At least there wasn't a boyfriend for me to leave, hm? That would have been even more awkward."

"You said you didn't have much luck with them, which I find entirely odd." He laughed, and it was a real one, some lightness in it, as he sat up.

I let go of his hand, playing with my glass again. It was easier to look out across the restaurant than at him. I didn't know if I could stand looking at his serious face, the weight of his hazel brown eyes. They were friendly eyes, always had been. If you looked closely, he had flecks of gold in the brown parts, a tell of the wolf within. I often wondered if that was why my eyes were their own bright blue, the fire in me creeping out however it could. Foolish ideas.

"Seemed unfair to get too serious with anyone when I knew I'd be leaving. I've gone on dates and the such, seen someone for a few months, but nothing… substantive, shall we say," I said.

"You never let any of them in?"

"Not anything serious. I had a business to run, it takes up so much time. And there were other things to consider. They make it harder for anything more than a casual fling, someone fun for a while."

"Other things?"

I shook my head at his question, resisting the urge to roll my eyes. "The same as you, no doubt. I'd bet you weren't evaluating potential girlfriends with one eye on telling them why you have to dip out on certain nights."

He shrugged, shaking his head. "You're right; I'm the same. I had a few girlfriends, but nothing that would make me reconsider us."

Us. That was such a simple way to sum it all up. Us. Not 'arranged marriage', not 'promised', not 'dead people chose this'. Us. I shook myself out of my bitter musings, tapping my watch. "We should make tracks. It's getting later."

"You don't want dessert?"

"I mean, I do, but the drive."

"I already did it once today; I don't mind fifteen minutes to get dessert. You had a sweet tooth, I remember."

I chuckled, leaning my head down on his shoulder for a beat. "What a silly thing to remember."

"That you like sweets?"

"Yeah. I remember other stuff about you."

"I look forward to finding out what it is." He waved to call the waitress over, shifting back to his own seat opposite. I felt the absence of his body like a breeze over my side.

CHAPTER 6

One sticky toffee pudding later, we were on the way back to his house, driving in what was now the full dark. The headlights cut a clean beam in the night's gloom, showing the cats' eyes on the road, and we drove in a comfortable silence.

"I have to ask something before we reach the houses. You won't like it," Seb said.

Oh boy. "Right. What is it?"

"What are you going to say about your magic?"

"Easy. I don't practice."

"Kat."

"I don't." I shot him a glare, which he ignored in favour of keeping his eyes on the road. Sensible, really.

"Your fantastic reflexes aside, we both know what happened earlier."

"I am not trained. My mother made sure I knew enough to be safe, and nothing more. I can't do much other than protect myself with fire."

He sat with that, clicking his tongue. I let the silence sit until I felt like it would crush me, filling the small space in the car. He cracked first. "So you have the innate ability, you're just untrained."

"Yes, as you saw."

"But you trained until your father died."

"Yes."

"Right." He nodded to himself. "So if I jump out at you and scream 'boo', you won't set me on fire?"

"I won't set you on fire anyway, because for some weird reason, it doesn't burn you. Which is terrible, may I add. Does it burn other wolves?"

"I think so. Your fathers did, so let's assume yes. I don't think anyone will volunteer to play test subject."

"Fair. Alright, so we will assume I am sufficiently robust to set fire to other wolves. That's it. No land blessings, no fertility blessings, none of the things my father used to do."

Seb looked over at me, fingers gripping the wheel tight enough I heard the leather squeak. "Pardon?"

"The rituals. He never explained too much, I was young, so I presume he was keeping it age appropriate. But I know he was involved in blessings. I can't do those."

"Right." He looked back out in front and blinked a few times. "Right, that's fine. We don't really do those anymore. So that's no problem. You being able to defend yourself will be enough."

"That's good to know. Your mother won't be disappointed?"

"No, no, she'll just be happy we got you back with the pack. Mostly unharmed. How is your chest feeling?"

"It's fine. I might have some more painkillers before I sleep, but it's not as sore as I expected."

"Good, that's good." He kept his eyes on the road, brows down low again, and I let the silence sit between us once more. He was clearly disappointed I wasn't trained, but at least he didn't see me as totally useless. There wasn't much more I could do about that.

We reached the little smattering of houses close to eleven, not too delayed by our dalliance at the restaurant. It was different from when I was a youngster but still recognisable as their little hamlet—a few new houses, and the road significantly improved by being tarmacked.

"Someone invested in the road."

"My idea. We were tearing up the gravel every summer," Seb said.

I grinned at him, nodding a little. "Smart man. It's not cheap though."

"Tell me about it. There was an entire argument about the upgrade costs, to see if we should tarmac or go for that reinforced gravel. I won in the end."

"Won by debate or wolf combat?"

"Debate, thank you." He shook his head as he pulled up to park, letting the engine die as he turned to face me. "Most of the pack will be home for the evening, so I'll make your introductions tomorrow. Is that alright?"

"Of course. It's late. I don't expect you to go knocking on doors."

He laughed, taking one of my hands between his. “Some would. They would demand the full traditional welcome. I can’t give you that right now, when it’s all up in the air, but I will later.”

“Good thing I’m not them, then. It’s fine. Is this the same house your mother and sister are in?”

“No, this is ours now. My mother wanted me in the official residence as soon as possible. I think it was more so she didn’t have to be here, really, but it only seemed right to do as she wished.”

“Right. Just us then.” I tried my best to keep my voice level. It wasn’t as if he was a stranger. We’d shared spaces before when we were kids, but that was a long while ago and it didn’t feel the same with him driving me here. Playing prince charming.

“There’s plenty of spare rooms, Kat. You’ll have space. It wouldn’t be proper for anything else until the wedding, anyway.”

My worries extinguished at that, because I trusted him, even if this was all strange. “That’s considerate.”

“Thank you. Come on, I’ll give you a refresh tour.”

We got out of the car together; me opening my door given we were safely within pack territory. If anyone was watching us here, there were bigger problems than us being seen to court each other.

“Who’s waiting up for you?” I pointed to the nearest window, a lamp on in the darkness.

"There shouldn't be anyone." Bastian frowned at the window, as if that would help the matter, and put a hand on my wrist. "Stay here. I'll check it out."

"Excuse me?"

"Just stick by the car. You can get back in and lock it if need be."

As if I'd be sitting here waiting for one of us to get knifed after earlier in the evening. "Alright, Lancelot, how about we both go? You can shout boo and I'll set someone else on fire."

"Fine. But stay behind me."

CHAPTER 7

Staying behind him had involved us doubling back on ourselves, Seb taking me to the back door so he could slip in through it like a thief in the night and move past the kitchen with no lights on. This was fine and well for him, who knew the house now it was different to over a decade ago, but I had to stay plastered to his back so I didn't kick a stool or slam myself into a newly placed counter.

The door through to the rest of the house was open a crack, enough to let the low light slip in and paint a beacon for us to aim for, but I held onto the hem of his shirt so I didn't give us away.

"Are you scared?" His voice was a whisper, barely enough to make out in the oppressive silence. I could hear the electricals in the room humming, and somewhere off to the depths of the room a clock was ticking.

"Only of giving us away."

"Just stick with me." Seb led us to the door, creaking it open more with agonising care as he frowned into the gap. His whole demeanour shifted, shoulders slumping as he muttered, "Oh, for goodness' sake."

"What?"

"Nothing, come on." He caught my hand in his, pulling the door open as he stepped through. "Daniel, what the hell is this?"

He tugged me into a cosy, open living room, which held what I could only say was a nest at the centre. A massively oversized sofa–easily a six-seater-was pulled away from the wall and towards the middle of the room, with dozens of cushions and a sea of blankets layered over the main cushions in rumpled piles. Candles dotted around the edges of the room, giving a hazy light, and what looked like roses were bundled into an obviously repurposed jug.

It was enchanting.

Stood beside it, looking terribly out of place and equally uncomfortable, was a man who I used to call little Daniel. He was easily six-four now, and broad as a shire horse, his shoulders low and square against the jut of muscle at his neck. The black vest he was in showed off his arms, muscled and running with ink that stood stark against his pale skin, though I couldn't see properly what the tattoos were. His hair was shorn short, a faint buzz of blond catching the candlelight, and his face was red enough to light a candle off.

We came to a stop a little outside of the glow of the nest, the sandalwood perfume of the candles mixing around us like a friendly cat.

"Well?" Bastian prompted.

"I didn't think you'd come in the back door, boss. I was going to leave when I heard the front door open."

"While that's very illustrative of your intentions, I repeat, what is that?" He pointed to the couch, and I bit my lip to stifle a laugh.

"Don't be a horror, Seb. Hey, Daniel." I gave Daniel a little wave, smiling at him as I stepped around Seb. "You got tall."

"Grew the bones myself," he said. He opened his arms for a hug, squeezing me like he had to check I was real when I stepped into it. "Long time since we saw you, Kat. I was worried you were going to tell him where to go."

"I am standing right here," Seb said.

"I'm glad to see you again," I said, ignoring Seb's comment. "All this fuss for me?"

He pulled back from the hug, looking at the sofa with a sheepish grin. "I figured you'd like a little den. I know you were young when you left, but a den's always good, isn't it?"

"I didn't know you were such a romantic." I looked back at the layers of blankets and cushions; clearly a cosy space made even more welcoming.

"I didn't either, or else I would have told Marie to keep an eye on you," Seb said.

"You were going to collect her with news of a body, Seb, didn't seem the most romantic." Daniel still talked out of the side of his mouth when he was uncomfortable. I could see the way his lips pinched together at the opposite end. It was sweet to think he'd remembered the early spring months we would spend as children, building little secret points in the woods or each other's houses, to doze in or read when the weather was too unpredictable or people too loud. We'd had a great time being free to do as we liked.

The kindness twisted in my chest like that knife would have done, but I couldn't find it in myself to say it truly hurt.

"Well, I'm not very good at romantic either, so he would have been pretty safe there," I said. I turned to look at the two of them, careful to hold my core rigid so I didn't upset my cuts. "It's a lovely thought, Daniel, thank you. Even if you were going to give him credit."

Seb wrinkled his nose, rubbing a thumb along the edge of his jaw before he spoke. "Yes, it's nice that you were going to do that. And not leave lit candles around to potentially burn the house down."

"That's why I was still here, fire safety and all that," Daniel said.

"Sensible," I added.

"Right, well now I've thoroughly ruined the romantic moment, can you get gone so I can get Kat settle in?" Seb said.

"You don't want me to help carry bags in, since I'm here?" Daniel nodded to the door, perking up.

"There's not that many. I packed light since…" I trailed off and looked at Seb, who dropped his head.

"What?" Daniel asked.

"Since we're going to be sorting out what happens with my shop, so I'll be able to pick up more things in a few trips," I said, in a rush. "I've had that shop five years. I need to be sure it's handled well while I'm away. All the drive up, I've talked his ear off on the way over about it."

"Oh yeah, he said you had a bookshop. I looked up your website. It's a bit old." Daniel laughed, shaking his head. "We can get one of the younger ones to hook you up with something better? I mean, Seb will sort all of that anyway, but my cousin Karin is big into coding. She'd love a chance to do something as an experiment, even."

"That would be awesome, yeah." I looked to Seb, who was now examining one rose like he wanted it to burst into flames like the surrounding candles. "If that's alright? I don't want to come in and start shoving things around."

"It would be good." Seb looked up at me with a grin, nodding. "The girls are good at coding. Getting their teeth into a proper project would help their confidence. They can use it in a portfolio too, later on."

Daniel nodded, happy as a lamb. "Great. I'll get back to Marie then. Let me know tomorrow what we're doing for a welcome party."

"Before you go, there's something else. Kat, come here." Seb motioned me over, setting an arm on my shoulder. "I'm not going to tell everyone, but someone attacked Kat at home. The guy got away. She saw him off just like a member of the pack would, but they're clearly making moves. Keep Marie and my mother safe, alright?"

"Yeah, no problem. You alright, Kat?" Daniel came half a step closer, his entire face tight.

"Some idiot with a knife thought he could get the better of me, like that was going to happen." I snorted a laugh, linking my arm over Seb's back, so I pressed into his side. "Not like he'd get through Seb anyway, is it?"

"No, no chance in hell. But that's not good. Should we have someone attached, in case?" He looked at Seb, all levity gone as he frowned between us.

"We'll see in the morning. We can have a proper discussion with everyone."

"Okay, as you say, boss." Daniel stepped back again, swinging himself around to head for the front door. "I'll get what there is in the car. You take care of Kat."

"What was that?" I asked as Daniel disappeared through the front door. "Suddenly cuddly?"

"What was your comment about the shop?"

"I was covering in case you didn't want to talk about the attacker. Clearly, people are expecting something." I nodded to the nest. Den. Whatever.

Seb rolled his eyes. "There was an anticipation of some happiness. People are excited about a wedding, some good news after the bad. They've missed you.

Your website could do with an update, though. It's clunky."

"Oh, you can shut up and—" A knock at the door cut me off before I could build up steam in, both our heads swivelling to the door.

"Sorry to call past late." Victor was standing in the doorway, left open by Daniel as he unloaded the car.

Victor was older than I remembered, the five years harder on him than they should have been. While he was still well put together, he looked worn for a man in his early fifties, his brown hair now streaked with silver at the temples and the crease at his forehead present even when he smiled. "I heard a commotion so wanted to see things were alright."

"Victor, hello." I stepped away from Seb, going over to offer my hand. "I think I owe you an apology from the last time we spoke."

"Oh yes, the threat of death by coffee if I came back." He smiled, taking my hand and instead of shaking it, pulling me into a hug. The jolt forward made my chest lurch, the skin stinging, but the noise I made died against his shoulder as he enveloped me in an embrace. "Don't worry about it, our little witch. You were grieving. We all know more about that now than we did."

"I didn't expect you to be so enthusiastic about Kat's return." Seb came closer, a hand on my shoulder as Victor released me from the spontaneous embrace. I let Seb draw me back to him, his arm around my shoulder again.

Victor nodded, glancing into the room and eyes lighting up at the sofa nest. "It's good for the pack to see things moving forward. You in the main house, with your mate, that's an eye to the future. It'll help settle things."

"It might not be that rosy. There was someone at Kat's house when we got there. Armed."

"Are you hurt?" Victor looked at me, stepping closer again. Wolves had never been huge on personal space, but this was a touch much.

"Seb saw the guy off, but I got a slight cut." I tapped the top of my chest, at the smaller cut, shrugging it off. "Nothing worse than everyone else is going through, I'm sure."

Victor frowned even as he nodded. "We'll make sure you have someone handy in case you need it. I know you'll be able to protect yourself like your father could, but we should stick together when there's a threat around."

"We will." Seb pressed a kiss to my temple, making my spine straighten. "You stay here a second, beautiful. I want to grab a word with Daniel before he goes."

"Sure." I smiled as he moved away, letting my hand linger on his arm. Evidently, we were keeping up appearances.

"You look good, Kat. Better than when I last saw you," Victor said.

"Thank you. I was very worn down when you visited. I'm sorry again."

"Not at all, petal, not at all. After Michael passed away, I got more of an appreciate for the hunger grief has. It's a cruel thing."

I blanched, a heavy weight plummeting in my stomach. Michael was Victor's son, an absolute clone of the man when he was younger, and they'd been as close as any parent and child I'd known. Rough as Victor could be, he had adored Michael. "I didn't know he had passed. I'm so sorry." Hesitantly, I set a hand on his elbow, unsure how much contact would be too much. We'd already hugged.

"No, Bastian won't have been able to catch you up on things yet. That will be a task for tomorrow, not late at night when you're first back with us." He glanced towards the front door, leaning a little closer. "It was a motorbike accident that took him a year ago. To lose him and then John so close together, it's a hard blow, but Bastian is a suitable heir for the pack."

"Doesn't stop you missing your son, though. That's horrible for you, Victor. I'm so sorry."

"It's kind of you to say. You know grief better than a lot of us, of course." He stepped closer, enough that I could feel the heat from his skin when he whispered his next comment. "Does he know you're untrained?"

"Yes." I set a hand on his shoulder, pushing back slightly, but he didn't move. "I've told him I can't do the rituals. He's fine with it."

"Good. The pack needs open and honest leadership. I'm sure it will not be too much of a disappointment for everyone." He pulled back, smiling at me again as he cupped my elbow. "I know it must be overwhelming to be back, Kat. You've been on your own for so long. Too long. It's not right that we didn't ask you back when your mother died. If you ever need to come and talk, I'm here. I'm not Bastian's father, but I know the pressures he's facing, and I know how much of a strain it can be for both sides of a couple. Don't be a stranger."

"Thank you." I tugged my arm free just as Seb came back in the door, smiling over at him as he set the case and bags down beside the sofa. "I thought Daniel was helping you?"

"I told him to head back home, given we had other company. Come on, I'll give you the updated tour."

"I'll take my leave, meantime. I look forward to the proper reintroduction tomorrow. Kat." Victor leaned in and pecked my cheek, ducking his head in a slight bow to Bastian before he left.

CHAPTER 8

Seb led me up familiar steps now covered in an unfamiliar carpet, much less worn through than when I'd last been here. The house was full of minor changes, new layouts and updated fashions, but it still felt familiar as the steps near the top creaked.

"So how is Victor doing?" I asked as we climbed up them, my bags in Seb's hands.

"He's been a substantial source of strength for the pack. It's been a hard year for him."

"He mentioned Michael had died."

"Yes. He still has Annabelle, but it's a lot for him to shoulder."

"Annabelle? I thought he was married to Rose?"

"Yes, Rose is his wife. Annabelle is his little girl." He paused at a door, glancing over his shoulder at me. "She's eleven this year. She must have arrived after you left."

"I don't remember the pregnancy."

"You had a thing or two happening." He gave a little shrug. "We'll get you caught up soon. Don't worry."

Easy for him to say. "Thanks. It will be good to see everyone, I suppose."

"You suppose?"

"I'm terrified, alright? Everyone has an impression of what this should be and I don't know what it is, and someone swung a knife at me recently. I'm not exactly collecting stamps on a frequent stabbing card." I would have crossed my arms over my chest if it wouldn't have hurt. At least I'd remembered that before I moved too much.

Seb turned, resting his back on the wall so he could look me over. "Would this be the first stamp if you were?"

"Oh, shut up." I shoved his shoulder, but there was no actual heat behind it, and he laughed at me. "And no, it wouldn't, but that doesn't mean I want to get the full collection. What's the prize at the end? You get your own knife to stab back?"

He snorted, the smile on his face almost like the one he had in the car. I liked that on him, the easy crinkle at his eyes when he was relaxed. "I think you'd be good with a knife."

"Oh, yeah?"

"Your tongue's this sharp. I bet you're even better with a blade."

I rolled my eyes at him, one hand planted on my hip. "Just because you get claws once a month."

"You could keep a knife the whole month."

"Sure, I'll check the kitchen and take my favourite." I peered around him. The door was closed, the dark-stained wood shiny from polishing. "Isn't this your room?"

He sucked air through his teeth, his head bobbing a little as he weighed up his words. "In a sense. I thought you would appreciate your own space until we get closer again. This used to be my room, but I've moved into a different one now."

"You don't want us in the same bed?"

"Not until the wedding. We'll have to share a room after that, but we can be proper until then." He caught the handle, turning from the wall to lead the way in.

The room was not as I remembered it. When we'd been kids, his room had been dark blue, with a selection of movie posters and books and an ever disastrous pile of clothes which often threatened to swamp whoever in our little bundle had been nearest. That had been until thirteen, before the kick of puberty and the formalisation of things stared somewhere off in the background. After that I'd been in Marie's room, never his, and he'd been much too busy with the other teen boys learning their dual-place, wolf and man.

Now the room was a breezy spring green, the light walls accompanied by an even lighter heather purple ceiling, which was perilously close to being nice, and the furniture was distinctly older. The wood was black stained, oak if I were to care to guess, and with a swooping realisation I realised I knew it.

"This is from our old house." I stepped around Seb, grateful when he flicked the lights on, so I could go up to the dresser. It was the one we had at home, in our little cottage, before we left.

"Well, I thought it might be some comfort. I thought that even before you said you weren't so keen to marry me, really, so it seems even more likely now. I know it's not much of a room, but it might feel safer than the other option."

"The other option being your bed?"

He gave that same little shrug. "Yes. The master bedroom is mine now, as master of the house. So they say."

I turned to look at him, in the room now and setting my bags down on the sizeable bed. That was new, at least, king sized with contrast sheets and covers on it like it should belong in a very nice hotel. "What do you mean?"

"The house still feels like it's my parents. I feel more like a caretaker than a master." He looked around the room before his eyes settled on me.

I stepped closer, taking his hand. "It passes. I felt the same about the apartment my mother and I shared at first. It's not been long yet. Just give yourself a little time to get used to it."

"Did you?"

"No, I bought my little house in Avon-on-Lee, but that was because I wanted to move out of the city." I glanced around the room; my tongue heavy in my mouth as I tried to think about the better parts. "It was a good place for us together, but I couldn't stay. So I got to make my little house as I wanted. You'll be able to do the same here. It will take time. And a little help, maybe."

"Maybe?"

"I don't think you'll be hurting for ideas, but you'll want to keep a sense of the family. Family can help with that."

"We should speak about family." Seb gestured for me to come closer and sat on the bed.

"On the bed, really? Is this another smooth move?"

"Kat."

"What? I'm fine stood up, thank you." I nearly crossed my arms at that. Something about the easy spread of his legs as he sank onto the edge of the mattress ruffled me unreasonably. It was so natural to have him there, despite how insane the evening had been.

"Alright. Do you know how long it is until the full moon?" I shook my head, trying to picture how the moon had looked when I last saw it. It wasn't out when I was walking home this time of year, the summer light enough to wander back safely.

"I haven't seen her in a while. Walking home isn't dark yet."

"Fair. I suppose you wouldn't be tracking it. Three days, it's the full moon."

"Three days. Including today?"

"Yes."

So, two days. The day after tomorrow. My chest tightened at the realisation, my ribs suddenly constricting when I caught Seb's meaning. "So we get married in two days?"

"Yes."

"Right." I sat down at that. Not beside him on the bed. I drew the chair out from the dresser I was standing beside, and sank into it. The tug of my longer cut prompted a stupid thought, which escaped before I could stop it. "I won't be able to wear an open-necked dress, then."

He laughed; his eyes bright in amusement. "No, not really. If I'd stopped that guy sooner, you would have more options. I'm sorry."

"Not your fault." The way my blood rushed in my ears wasn't so different from when I'd been attacked. It was like I could feel it moving through me, the rush and pull of it as I tried to rationalise what he had said. "Two days."

"It's sudden, I know. But there are expectations. And while you are at risk, until we figure out what happened to my father, it is better they see us doing what's expected."

I nodded. There was a logic to it. And men in my house with knives. Better to be here. "Well, I don't have a good enough dress for that. I'll need to go into town and find something."

"Marie will be delighted to go with you. Are you alright?"

"I hadn't thought it was so soon."

Seb stood up and came to me, kneeling so he was before me. One hand went to my knee, the other tilting my chin so he could catch my eyes. He had such serious eyes. "I'm sorry, beautiful. I should have brought it up sooner, but with the attack."

"I understand." I gave the nicest smile I could. It didn't feel like much on my face, but he smiled back. It suited him. For a silly moment I wanted to cup his cheek, run the pad of my thumb over the swell of his cheekbone, but I shoved the thought away. "Are there plans already?"

"Some. My mother wants to talk them through with you. She feels it should be a joint matter, so that your wishes are considered as well." His hand dropped, finding mine to squeeze it. "I'd like you to say what you do and don't like, too. I have no idea if you have strong feelings about it, but if you do, we'll make it work."

"Strong feelings like we shouldn't do this? Everyone who negotiated this is dead, Seb. You don't have to go through with it."

He sighed, his gaze dropping for a beat. "I know that's what you think. But the promise has been longstanding, and to go back on it would be seen as not only weak, but an insult to the dead. We have to do it, even if it's temporary. At least until we're all safe."

An insult to the dead. I mulled that phrase around, swirling it like wine in a glass. I knew enough about the dead to think it was a trite sentiment, but that might have been my bitterness again. It was more like rotten fruit than a rich bouquet, and it would stain my teeth if I didn't keep it at a distance. "Is there a big thing for wolf divorce?"

He looked back up at me, jaw working a little before he answered. "We have it, yes. If someone needs to leave a partner, especially if there are children involved, there are ways of doing it. I don't want you to need to do that, but it exists."

I grabbed onto that like a lifejacket, a lurid flash of hope. "Right. Right, so we can do this and there are still choices later. Neither of us will be stuck."

Seb shook his head, squeezing my hands again. "No, Kat. Neither of us will be stuck. I don't want to trap you or anything like that. There are some other things we should talk about, but…" He sighed, wrinkling his nose. "Maybe tomorrow. It's nearly midnight. Can I check your cuts before I leave you be? I imagine you're fit to drop."

"I am tired, yeah. You that keen to see me topless again?"

If that was colour on his cheeks, I would do him the decency of pretending not to notice it. "I don't remember you being this mischievous."

"You don't remember me much then. I've always had a mouth on me."

"One that used to shout and scream, not sass me."

"That's because you ran off with the other lads. I've been fluent in sarcasm since I was a teen."

"We ended up spending a lot of time separate, didn't we?" He turned away, a hint as much as I knew one, and I pulled my top up and folded it onto my lap.

"You can look back."

He turned and frowned. I glanced down to where he was looking and saw a blush of red through the dressing - only a few smatterings on the upper one, but the lower had a line of dark red, like the wound had opened again. "I'll change that."

"I can do it, if you're tired too."

"Nonsense. I know where everything is. Sit tight and I'll be back shortly." He stood up, giving me a soft smile before leaving the room. The step at the top squeaked as he descended, leaving me in the room with my thoughts.

It was a pleasant room, really, there'd obviously been care put into making it look good for someone, and given the furniture I expected it was for me. It was almost sweeter than Daniel's attempt at romance. There was a kindness to both, a funny sort of charm, that I hadn't known since we left the pack.

Still, a creeping chill of unease ate up my spine, making my skin prickle and the fine fuzz on my arms stick up. Not quite the same as a wolf, but it made me laugh even as I rubbed the skin to settle the goosebumps off. I stood up, drifting around the room as if one piece of furniture would hold some secret, some quick little detail that would make all of this make sense.

No such luck, just memories. At least they made me smile. I looped around to the bed, sitting on the far side of it and feeling the mattress. It was firm, with some good bounce to it, and I flopped backward onto it. It would be easy to close my eyes and drift off.

The squeak on the stair made me sit up, shaking my head to dispel the intoxicating tendrils of fatigue.

"Are you that beat?" Seb asked, smiling at me from the door. He looked a little softer around the edges now, a couple of buttons undone on his shirt, the sleeves rolled up. It was a pleasant view.

I covered my mouth to yawn, nodding at him. "I didn't realise I was, but yes. It caught up to me suddenly. I blame the very nice mattress."

"Quite the testimonial. I'll not take too long at this then. Lie down again, if you like, and I'll give you peace once this is done."

"Thanks, Seb."

"No problem, beautiful."

CHAPTER 9

Morning came in a rush of bad dreams and sweat covered skin, the cover tangled around my legs as I sat up in fright. It was dark, and I fumbled for a switch to click the lamp on. Soft white light flooded the room, and grabbing my phone, I saw it was just before five. My heart yanked against my ribs like an unruly colt, the pain quicksilver between my ribs. It was okay. I was alright.

I put my fingers up to my throat, caught the chase of my pulse, the tack of sweat still drying over my racing blood. Dropping my head, I scrubbed my hands over my face, as if to shake the dreams away. It was not as if these were my first nightmares. Just being in a new place, that wasn't really new, and having been attacked last night. Nothing but an adrenaline hangover.

I rolled out of bed, padding into the small en suite. Glancing in the mirror, I looked grim: pale skin, dark eyes, hair wild. Certainly not what someone wanted to see about their future bride. Maybe I would have to get some better makeup when we went looking for a dress. I was sure Seb would stretch to that. I laughed at the ridiculousness of it as I turned the shower on, grateful it wasn't too loud.

Stepping into the water, I soaked under it for a few minutes, breathing in the steam and letting my hands skim over my skin. It was grounding to feel the parameters of my body, the length of my limbs: I was here. I was fine.

I peeled the dressings off my chest, turning my body away so I could let the water roll around the surrounding skin before getting back under the stream. It stung, and I kept my shoulders stooped to prevent the water from hitting the cuts directly, but the skin didn't seem inflamed and other than some ugly scabs, it was looking better than yesterday. Good. It would probably scar. My skin usually did, but it wasn't terrible. With the right oils there wouldn't be much to see.

After I washed up and conditioned my hair, I stepped out of the shower, wrapping myself up in a towel and tipping forward to encircle my hair in a separate one. Twisting water out of it, I span the towel in on itself, standing with a tip of my head so the towel went up and over, lying down my back. It balanced there as I dried myself off, then went back into the bedroom. I had brought a bundle of clothes with me, enough to stay for a while, and I flipped the case lid open to look through them.

Glancing out at the window, it was still coming properly light, but it was nice. Mild. I fished out a set of shorts, sleeping ones rather than proper running ones, and a tank top. I would go a jog around the woods, get rid of the lingering sense of being out of place, and I could be back in before breakfast. It would be an easy way to see what was new in the little smattering of houses, too. The pack houses were hardly a village, there weren't enough to earn a proper shop, but there were enough of them crowded together that it was their own distinct space. It would be good to get to know it again before I married in.

I grimaced at the thought, tossing the towel off my hair to comb it out. I put it in a high braid, twisting the hair tight together so I would have some nice curls when I let it out later. May as well try to look nice. If the hoody I grabbed was tattered and well worn, I'd blame it on packing in a rush.

~

The woods that surrounded the pack were thick and wild. Well set and away from the road, they teemed with the buzz of life—birds and bugs, the occasional skitter of hooves which I presumed to be deer. There had been deer before.

I jogged through a rough path, not exactly a trail but more worn than the rest of the forest floor. Some of it was uneven, needing me to slow down to avoid snagging roots or the shaky give of over dry mud that crumbled away, sinking low enough that I had to tug myself free. I tied the arms of my hoodie around my waist after the second time, giving into the inevitable trickle of sweat down my temple. At least there had been no midges.

After fifteen minutes, I found myself in a large clearing, the circle within easily as big as a school playing field. The grass was crushed, twisted this way and that from a lot of previous activity before, and at a few spots I could see dark plastic boxes with heavy padlocks on them.

I relaxed as I recognised them, stretching my neck out and settling my shoulders. This was a turning spot, somewhere where members of the pack could come and change with privacy. I'd seen a few, though never quite this big, before we left. It was good that they'd got a bigger one, which was getting used if the boxes were what I suspected: spare clothes, a space for snacks and water bottles for anyone tired after the shift.

I wandered over to one of them, kneeling to inspect the lock. It was well maintained, oiled and clean, and I would bet well stocked inside from the noises it made with a firm shake. A good safety measure, something to keep the pack hale if they were running through the woods at night.

They'd be needed shortly. I did not know how that would work for the wedding, actually. Seb would have to change, at least at some point. There'd be the full moon. Would we be married in the day? The evening, more likely, I remembered that from being younger–the kids allowed to stay up for the main ceremony and ushered away for the rest. I'd need to find out if it was still the same.

I sat, heavily, on the plastic box, my stomach tight at the thought.

A gasp sounded behind me and I twisted on my seat, catching sight of a little girl in the trees less than ten feet away. She was still as a deer, her mouth quivering as she looked at me. Enormous eyes, dark as tree bark, and long blonde hair which shone in the morning light. She wore little more than pyjamas. I couldn't see her feet, but she was shivering.

"You okay there, sweetheart?" I asked. She shook her head, wrapping her arms around herself. "What's wrong?"

"I don't know where I am." She looked ready to cry, her little shoulders bunched up around ears.

"You're in the woods. It's very early though. Did you come out here on your own?"

"I don't know. I went to bed last night and now I'm here." She cried, her lip wobbling over into a sad grimace.

"Hey, come here, it's alright. Can you come here?" I held an arm out and she launched herself into my side, nearly tipping me over off the box. "What's your name?"

"Annabelle."

The name rang like a bell in my mind as I hugged her back. "Is your daddy Victor?" She nodded, blinking up at me. She had an awful pretty face, still round with puppy fat on the cheeks, but she'd grow into being a beauty like her mother. "I know Victor. He's friends with some of my friends."

"I don't know you."

"No, you won't. I've not been here for a long while. But I know Bastian, and I know Daniel and Marie, and I used to know your mother, too."

"I'm not supposed to trust strangers, but you smell like the pack."

"That's okay. You don't have to trust me when you've only just met me." She wasn't as cold as I expected, which was good, meant she couldn't have been out that long. Her feet were bare, though, and she shivered against me as she pressed tighter.

"I want to go home."

"We can do that then. Here, why don't you put this on?" I lifted my hips up, tugging my hoodie free. "It'll be huge on you, but it's got to be warmer than your jammies."

She looked at it, then sniffed it a little. Seemingly satisfied, she pulled it over her head; the hood crumpling around her until I tugged it back. "Thanks."

"No problem. Is it coming up to your first turn?"

She nodded, rolling the sleeves up a little. "Dad says I'll turn soon. Maybe this month, maybe next. I hope it's this month."

"Yeah?"

Her brows came together as she nodded, a stern line of pale blonde. "I want to run around with everyone."

"Is that why you're here, at the turning spot?"

"I don't know. I didn't mean to be out here." She looked stricken, twisting on one leg.

"That's okay. I had a friend who used to sleepwalk when she was little, and she'd do all sorts. Eat food from the fridge, or stack things up in the middle of a room. It happens sometimes. Are you hurt at all?" I had seen no blood on her clothes, but she was dirty, like she'd fallen.

"No, I want to go home."

"We can do that. I'm going to take you back the way I came, because I don't know the woods so well anymore. Is that alright?"

She nodded, looking the way I came. "That's a good way to go."

"Great. Now, do you want me to give you a piggyback since you don't have any shoes?"

"Would you?" She perked right up at that, blinking at me.

"Sure. I have a bookshop back at home so I'm used to lifting things. I bet you don't even weigh as much as a box of hardbacks."

She giggled at that, a little sparkle in her eyes. "That's silly."

"I know, but you've got to be a little silly to have some fun. And life's much better with a little fun." I winked, standing up.

"You're good with kids." A man's voice came across the clearing, and I stepped in front of Annabelle as I turned to look for the owner.

A man was standing at the far end of the clearing, close to where I'd come in. He was taller than me, nearly Daniel's height, and something about the way he looked us over made my spine stiffen.

"Annabelle, do you know who that man is?"

"No," she whispered.

"Okay. Just stay by me then. Have you been there long, sir?"

"Sir? That's very formal." The man stepped into the clearing, walking lazily closer. He was casually dressed, dark blue jeans and an open shirt that showed a white vest underneath it, and scuffed up boots on his feet. He was thickset, his shoulders and arms well defined, and my stomach flipped at the smirk tugging at his lips. Sandy yellow hair, finer than most, straying towards white at some bits. He should look good, but everything about him made my skin itch.

"I don't think I know you. Seems appropriate to be polite."

"Hm, nice to know you have manners." He stopped a few feet from us, flashing an easy grin. He slid his hands into the back pockets of his jeans, leaning over a little to look us up and down. "Pretty little things, the pair of you."

"Are you lost?" I straightened my shoulders, shifting my weight on my hips. Annabelle hugged against the back of my legs like a shivering shadow.

"No, no, I know these woods pretty well."

A brief surge of anger skimmed across me, and I was 'pretty' certain though I didn't know him, I hated him. It was such an unnecessary obfuscation, giving nothing, and something about the way he had stalked forward made me want to bare my own teeth. "Do you have business with the Weirs?"

"Now, how do you know that name, pretty?"

I bristled at the comment, biting my tongue to keep the immediate response to myself. "I'm friendly with the family. And others."

"Are you now? Don't seem so friendly."

"I don't know you. And you're in their woods, and it's early. You don't exactly seem dressed for a jog."

"No, but you are." He looked up my legs. "You're bleeding though." He tapped the point on his chest.

"Someone was careless with a knife."

"Shame."

"He came off worse than me."

He ducked his head and laughed at that, his shoulders bouncing easily with the move, but when he looked back up, there was a glint in his eye. "I do so like blood."

"Sweetie, I need you to listen to me, okay?" I reached behind me to rub Annabelle's shoulder, giving it a little squeeze of reassurance. "Run back home and get your daddy for me. Now." I shoved her back towards the trees and stepped forward, squaring up to the man.

CHAPTER 10

His brows popped up as Annabelle fled. They were the same fine blond as his hair, and the smirk on his lips never shifted. "That was rude."

"So's scaring a child."

He sauntered a step closer, almost within arm's reach. "I don't seem so scary, do I? I'm not some big bad wolf."

"Just a regular one?"

"Know a lot about wolves, pretty girl?"

Yeah, I hated him. I smiled extra brightly, my teeth on show, gaze flicking to the edge of the treeline. I couldn't see anyone but him, and he'd clearly felt comfortable approaching. Either he had company, and he was the distraction, or he really thought he was that good. "Hard not to in these woods."

"You aren't one, though. None of the smell about you." He waved his hand in my general direction. I stepped back, the plastic box at my side. If I went back much further, I'd be in the woods, on the side I didn't know. Bad plan.

"No, I'm a different sort of thing. Do you have a name?"

"What will you give me for it?" He folded his arms, tilting his chin at me in what I was sure he thought was a sultry manner.

I scoffed at him, resisting the urge to cross my arms as well. Better to have them free, ready. I had options. "You're not some fairy creature. You don't need anything for your name."

"Maybe I want something, though."

"What would you want?"

"Your name in return."

"Just that?"

He made a show of considering it, his gaze settling on my chest. "How about some of your nice blood?"

"Oh boy, are you naturally like this or is this some act?"

He lolled his head to the side, eyes trailing up over me in a deliberate check over. "I will admit, I'm having a lot of fun. Which would you prefer?"

"I think I'd feel better if this was some bullshit, honestly."

He whooped a laugh, head coming back up. "Naughty. Why would you like that more?"

"Because otherwise there is a crazy man wandering around in the Weir woods and it's a full moon tomorrow. Doesn't seem like that's going to end well."

"Hm, you're right. That wouldn't be good for anyone. Easy to go missing in these woods."

"If you don't know the paths."

"Do you?" he asked.

"Why?"

"I'm trying to figure out what you are. Wandering around dressed so skimpy, snooping on things, cuddling lost children. She's a pretty little girl. Is her name really Sweetie?"

"No."

"Thought not. You're quite convinced I'm bad, aren't you?"

"I'm not seeing much evidence otherwise." I raised a brow at him, patience as thin as the scar that cut through one pale eyebrow. Might have been an old piercing.

"What would you do if I was? You're not going to get away from me. If I'm the big bad wolf, then you must be red riding hood, even if you gave your cloak away to her."

I laughed, shaking my head at him. "Let's drop that act, bud. Why are you here?"

"I followed you from the edge of the woods."

Wonderful, just what I wanted to hear. "Creepy, and that's not an answer."

"I wanted to see what idiot went jogging in wolf woods with no protection."

"Ah, you're assuming I have none. I can see why you'd make that mistake."

"What, you got a tazer hidden somewhere really surprising?"

I wrinkled my nose at the comment. "Don't be lewd, I don't know you and I don't have to put up with it. If you're not with the pack, you're making a mistake being here."

"Who says I'm not?"

"I can't see John taking much to you, no offence."

He sucked air through his teeth, giving a lazy shrug. "John's not here anymore. Someone killed him."

"But Bastian's taken up his place, and I know he wouldn't like you at all."

"Do you think so? I've been told I grow on people."

"Like mould, I bet."

He snickered, kicking one foot back onto the point of his toes. "You have quite a mouth on you for a human."

"And you have quite an ego for whatever you are."

"An obedient servant of the moon, I assure you. I could show you. If you like."

"I'd rather you didn't."

"Scared, pretty girl?"

"Not of you."

"Let's change that." He launched himself at me, too quick for me to hop the box to go aside, and shoved me back into one of the trees. My head hit the trunk, and I grunted in pain, his hand coming over my mouth to smother the sound.

I bit into his fingers to shake it off, earning a further push back into the tree. The spot I had bumped before flared with angry pain. My vision got a spiderweb lace of black for a moment, the rush of my pulse loud in my ears, but his smug face was enough to bring my focus back.

"Get off me." I snarled the words out, stilling when he set a hand up beside my head.

"Not so fast, baby. I just got close. I'm Josh, by the way." He leaned in so he pressed against me, hips snug to mine. Cocky bastard, I was going to yank some of that lovely hair out of his scalp.

"Charmed."

"Not yet, but I bet you will be soon. Do you know what happens if a werewolf bites a pretty little thing like you?" He stroked two knuckles against my cheek, face low and nearly touching mine.

"The Weirs don't do forced turning. They're not that sort of pack."

"I'm not with them, though." He shook his head, lips pursed in a false moue. "I bet you'd be just as pretty as a wolf as you are now."

"Do you think that's going to scare me?"

He dipped his head lower, taking a lick of the soft skin at the valley of my breasts. I cringed, setting my head back against the trunk, glowering at him as he pulled back up. "You taste scared. Blood and sweat, they always taste best together."

"You're boring me now." I'd had enough of this. Annabelle should be safely away, and I wasn't about to let him lay hands any further.

I smiled, taking a deep breath as I tried to settle my heavy pulse. He quirked his brow at me, that same smirk pulling up, and I shoved my head forward, hard, into his nose. My forehead got a splattering of fiery blood and he near howled, staggering back enough that I could peel myself from the bark and get back into the clearing, putting some distance between us.

It was a short won victory. I could hear him running after me, and while I tried to pivot out of his way, his bulk slammed into me from behind in a tackle that would have made an athlete proud. The air rushed out of my lungs at his weight over mine, my face crushed into the green beneath me.

Sucking in a breath, I screamed, kicking my legs out and writhing to try to get out from under him. He yanked my shoulder, twisting me over onto my back before planting his hips to straddle me.

"Now whose bitch are you to think you can pull something like that, hm?" I reached up to claw at his bloody face and he grabbed my wrists, pinning them above me. "I asked you a question."

"I'm nobody's but my own, and if you think a bloody nose is the worst I'll do to you, you're a damn fool."

"So feisty, I can't wait to break you in. Just wait until you see how much better it is when you've got the wild in your veins. Try not to look away." He leaned up, arcing his spine and throwing his head back. His eyes flooded dark, and when he looked down his face had started to change, a fine down of hair covering the skin which was melding towards the centre, elongating. I knew it, wolf.

"I don't think so." I dragged my knees up, planting my feet on the grass and twisting my hips to buck him sideways. He jolted, grip on my wrists loosening enough that I could reach up and grab his collar, get my fingers up against his neck. "Stay."

It was, on reflection, a touch bitchy to use a dog command to fuck with his change. I should've resisted the desire to give into my baser urges like that. He shuddered, gagging as the changes to his body reversed, and he tipped off of me like he was going to vomit.

"What did you do?"

"Kneed you in the balls." I rolled away from him, curling in on myself as my chest lurched in pain. I would never heal at this rate, the wound was angry and leaking red. My top was ruined too, unless Seb had some peroxide in the house. Maybe he would.

Josh's ragged breath sounded nearby, and I flinched away from a grab at my shoulder, yelping when his hand caught my high braid instead. He yanked me back towards him, ragged gasps hot in my ear.

"Liar. What did you do?" His face was a lurid red, I wasn't sure if that was rage or the effects of the magic. It rather complimented the blood smeared over his face. I tried to pull away, shoving at him - he was sluggish to bat my hands away, but his grip on my hair was solid.

"Why, are you scared? I thought you were the big bad wolf."

The slap sent a sudden flash of white across my eyes, my face turning before the pain even registered. I laughed, revelling in the sudden flare of heat and stinging across the left side of my face. "What are you?"

"I'm a bookshop owner, from a few towns over."

"Tell me!" He pulled my braid up and hit my head against the ground, the grass at least some form of cushion. My mind span, stomach twisting to empty itself though there was nothing there. I kept laughing, shoving up on my hip so I could spit the words at him.

"I don't know what to say, Josh. Lots of guys get performance anxiety their first time with someone new. Don't feel bad about it." I cracked into a wicked giggle, yelping when he slapped me again.

"If you don't tell me, I'll beat it out of you."

I had to get a hold of myself, the rush of magic and adrenaline was too much and I was leaning into the worse side of my tempter. I couldn't though, if he thought being such a dick would get something for him I wanted to disabuse that in the sharpest way possible. "Don't reckon that'll work. You'll never know what's happened if you kill me, though. Isn't that a bitch?"

"I'll choke it out of you if I have to." He grabbed my throat with one hand, shoving me down into the ground. "Tell me what you did."

"How can I if you choke me?" I regretted the comment as his grip tightened.

"Speak!" He brought his free fist up like he would punch me, and my fingers clenched with the beginning of fire. It was always a bit late to kick in, unruly compared to the other natural talent I'd been left with.

"Joshua, get your hands off her immediately!" A shout rocked through the clearing, before someone tackling him sideways barrelled Josh's weight off me.

"Kitty Kat, you okay?" Daniel was above me, the bulk of his body over me like a shield. "She's bleeding!"

I sighed, slumping back down into the grass. "It's mostly his blood."

"What?" That was Seb. I couldn't see him, past Daniel, but I knew the voice.

"Get off me, Weir." Josh sounded pained, and a dark, petty part of me enjoyed that.

"Did the girl get back, okay?"

"Yes, she told us what was going on," Daniel said. "Can you stand?"

"Yeah, I'm good. I'm alright." I patted his shoulder, taking the offered hand when he stood up and took me with him. My mind seemed to stay on the ground for a few seconds, standing feeling like I was moving in syrup, and I stumbled a little.

"Kathryn, are you injured?" Victor was beside us. It must have been him who shouted given where he'd approached us from.

I shook my head as I looked at him; the movement making me nauseous. I really did not want to throw up. "Is Annabelle okay? I didn't want her to see anything bad."

"She's fine, thank you." He smiled, squeezing my shoulder. "We should separate those two." He nodded over to the scrum of two bodies twisting against each other, the shock of Josh's hair showing tucked close in at Seb's ribs, fists being flung on both sides. They were hissing words at each other, but I couldn't make much out.

"I'll do it," Daniel said.

I winced, leaning on him. "I'll come too. I wound Josh up on purpose, I should do something to help."

"What?" Victor asked.

"I didn't want him going after Annabelle and I didn't know who he was. Still don't."

Daniel sighed. "He's Josh Munro. He's one of the rival pack."

"What?" There'd never been a rival pack. Victor had been the last rival, well before me or Seb or the rest of us were even around, and the peace had been brokered easily. From what we had been told.

"It's complex. We can discuss it on the way back home, but yes. Joshua is the second in command of the

Campbell pack. Which makes this entire situation disastrous," Victor said.

"Bit handsy for someone in that position."

"Undoubtedly. We will have to discuss that. Did he do anything… unchivalrous to you?" Victor asked. He glanced at my top, askew and marked with blood. I probably looked rough. So much for that shower.

I shook my head, tugging the back of my top so the neckline hiked up some more. "Not really, just the choking and slapping. Slamming me into a tree." Better not mention that lick.

"That motherfu—"

Victor put a hand on Daniel's arm. "Daniel, peace. We need to separate them before this escalates."

"Let's get on that." I turned to head towards the fighting men, flinching as I heard someone grunt in pain.

"Let me do it." Daniel went past me, jogging over to the two of them to grab a shoulder of each. He yanked them backwards, planting himself between Seb and Josh, facing Josh down with a grin that spoiled for a fight.

"You think you can lay hands on me like you're some bouncer in a club?" Josh growled, eyes on Daniel.

"Joshua, before you launch yourself into a fresh quarrel, can I take a moment of your time?" Victor breezed in, much closer to the man I knew than the twitchy whispers of last night.

Josh scowled. "What do you want, old man?"

"Do you know who that girl is?"

"Some stupid bitch wandering around the woods."

"Watch your mouth, Josh." Daniel flexed his shoulders, popping the knuckles on his left fist.

"Can we not swing our collective dicks, guys?" I stepped closer, tapping Seb's wrist so he knew I was near.

"You let her talk like that?" Josh scoffed, shoulders relaxing as he crossed his arms.

"She can speak how she likes." Seb slid his arm around me, low at my waist, so he could press us closer together. "She's my wife."

It was quite entertaining to watch Josh's mouth fall open, face wiping blank of his previous smirk. He glanced at me again, lips quirking a little, before he settled his gaze on Seb. "You're marrying her?"

"Tomorrow. And if she has bruising because of your actions, I'll give you matching ones next time we meet."

"I broke his nose. I think we're even," I said.

"You did more than that."

I shrugged. "I won't apologise for kneeing you in the balls. You were being a creep."

He frowned at me, working his jaw for a minute. I was walking a tight line here. Their pack would know I was a witch, that was never hidden when Seb and I were promised. He would recognise magic in what I had done to him. So he didn't need to comment on that, it would be the same as any mixed marriage, there was always magic. Magic for my protection. They didn't have to know what that extended to. I prayed he didn't tell them what I had done, or that really would put me in a pickle. I held my breath as he seemed to reach a decision.

"I didn't know someone had a claim on you. If I'd known that, we'd have had a different conversation." He gave a little duck of his head, as close as I imagined he got to deference.

"One where you didn't threaten to bite me?"

"What?" Seb went rigid beside me.

"A joke, just a joke. I wanted to scare her off. We don't need joggers and tourists around here. There's not a scratch on her from me. I didn't even punch her."

"You had your hands around her neck, Josh. I saw that." Seb's own voice was at a near growl, and I saw the flood of colour to his eyes - the edge of true aggression.

I pressed up on my toes so I could whisper in his ear, setting my hand on his opposite cheek. "Leave him, love. He's clearly in over his head."

Seb turned slowly to look at me, eyes tracking over my face. "What?"

"I don't need you to beat on someone weaker than you to show your strength. Let's head back." I pecked a kiss to his cheek, turning to look back at Josh. "I'm sorry we had such a poor first meeting. I hope we can both do better next time."

"I'd enjoy that. I'll look forward to seeing you at the wedding. Gentlemen." Leaping on my obvious bait Josh nodded to the others, then turned to walk away, disappearing off into the trees before anyone could respond.

"He's coming to the wedding?" I couldn't help the question. At least he'd look ugly in the photos.

"We must be seen to be open to negotiations. That means they have to join us with marking the event, even if we find it distasteful," Victor said.

Seb shook his head, sucking air through his teeth. "We won't have them. He had his hands around my wife's throat." A little thrill went through me at him using the phrase again, calling me his wife, despite my concerns. There was an open care in it that made my heart swoop.

I shook my head. "No, we should still have them, show we're better than them. Let's shame them with our hospitality."

"Did she used to be this evil?" Daniel asked with a laugh.

"She's clearly her father's daughter. It's wonderful to see." Victor smiled at me. "If you'll excuse me, I want to check Annabelle is well."

"Of course. We'll head back as well. Can you walk okay?" Seb turned me in his hold, hands on my shoulders so he could look me over. Victor disappeared into the woods, the opposite way Josh had gone, and the three of us were left together.

I put a hand to Seb's chest, to calm him as much as me. "I'm fine, Seb. Do you have a bath, though? I could really do with a soak." Now the fear had worn off, my body ached, the bruising and no doubt scratches at my back flaring with pain. My face wasn't much better, but that would fade off once my blood settled. His slaps were no worse than I'd had before. The jitters of adrenaline were also giving way to shivering, though, and I wanted to dunk myself into hot water to shed it all away.

"There's a bath in the master bedroom en suite. You can use that." Seb hugged me closer, crushing me into his chest as he wrapped his arms across my back. "Daniel, can you let the others know we're fine but there'll be a short delay. I want to check her wounds over."

"On it." Daniel gave a brief nod, scuffing my shoulder playfully as he went past.

"Did he hurt you?" I asked. Seb wasn't bleeding, but there had been fists thrown. It could have been more than it looked.

"Forget me. What did he do to you? I can smell him all over you, if he's done something unspeakable, I'll take his fucking skin."

"Seb, no." I wrapped my arms around him, holding him close. "He was all mouth. He sniffed at my blood, and made a show of being able to overpower me, but that's it. He didn't even change. I'm fine."

"Your neck is livid red." He said it into my hair, his chin tucked tight against me as he cupped the back of my head and pressed me impossibly closer. It was like he thought I'd vanish if he didn't touch me. I suppose I had, to him. I should have left a note about going jogging.

I sighed, letting go of him. He didn't release me, keeping me in place. "I, uh. He choked me too, yeah. Slapped me twice. Hit my head off that tree, I probably shouldn't fall asleep for a bit."

Seb growled, pulling back to look at me. "Are you joking?"

"No."

He turned to look at the treeline. "I'm going to kill him."

"Seb, no. If you want to do something, take care of me."

He frowned, tilting his head at me. "What do you mean?"

"You patched me up after the attack at my house. I liked that. It made me feel safe. Do that again, to settle me down. Yeah?"

The tight line of his lips didn't waver, but he nodded. "I'll always do that for you, beautiful. Though I make no promises about not harming Josh."

"Don't make me put it in the vows."

He snorted at that, pulling me in against his chest. "You're impossible. Here." He shucked off the shirt he was wearing, showing a tight top underneath. “Wear this. You’re shivering.”

CHAPTER 11

"We need to get you a bodyguard." The bath water was running, loud in the en suite, and Seb was taking up the entire doorway again as if someone would come through it. Never mind that he'd locked the bedroom door, and was a solid wall to block anyone else.

"Victor said the same last night. It's a bit much, no?"

"You've been attacked twice."

"I did goad Josh on to distract him while Annabelle ran off. He probably wouldn't have been so aggressive if I'd been less hostile."

"I don't know about that. Will doesn't keep tight enough hold of his second. He might have done it anyway."

Delightful. I trailed a hand through the water, testing the heat. "Is Daniel your second?"

"Yeah." He nodded, looking over his shoulder.

"Thought so. How long have him and Marie been a thing?"

Seb blew air out of his cheeks, tilting his head back to look at me. "Five years, give or take. How did you know they were together?"

"No one but Marie calls me Kitty-Kat, not since you and the boys ran off. Had to be he'd picked it up from somewhere. And you told him to look after her and your mother."

Seb nodded, peering over at the bath. There were a lot of bubbles, to be fair. I had chucked them and Epsom salts in to help the bruising. "You're not incorrect. I've always thought it was a sweet nickname. A bit twee for me."

"You'll have to find another one for me, then."

"You called me love, out in the woods."

"We have to sell the together thing, no?" I asked, smirking at him. "And if Josh is part of the rival pack, that will matter. If they think there's something wrong, they'll exploit it, I would guess."

"Yes." He nodded, his shoulders slumping a little. "It was easier when my father was negotiating. He could roar Will Campbell down like he was a kitten."

"You threatened to uninvite them from the wedding, and I nearly set their second on fire. I think you're in a good spot."

"Hm, about that. Why was it only nearly? You had the knife guy up in seconds."

"That was instinctual, at my house. This was more of a fight: less panic, no automatic fire. Which is good. We don't want magic fire all over everywhere."

"I don't think I would have minded Josh crispy."

I laughed, tried to ignore the pain it brought to my throat. "You're terrible. I'm fine. It wasn't a fun experience, and my everything hurts, but it could have been worse. I was more worried about the poor girl."

"Rose will take care of her. She's been sleepwalking a bit, happens with some of us before the first change."

"What a stress." The tub was full enough, so I turned the taps off, looking at Seb. He looked back. "Are you not going to go do something else while I bathe?"

"No." He shook his head, glancing back into the bedroom. "There are towels and a robe for you when you're done, and I've told Daniel to push things back. I'm all yours just now."

"Which is charming, but…." I looked at the bath again. "You're not getting in here with me."

"No, but I want to check your wounds. There are enough bubbles for modesty."

I blinked furiously at him, any chill I'd felt in the woods entirely lost as heat flooded my face. "You're going to hang around the bathroom while I wash?"

"I'm going to check your wounds over. And we should talk about things. I need to get you up to date on what's been happening with the rival pack, and how negotiations stand. You're expected to come along to them after tomorrow."

"Hurray. I bet it'll be as fun as delivery negotiations."

"I know, I know. I'm not keen either, but it is a requirement. Victor's doing what he can, but the pack looks weak without a full contingency. Are you going to get in?" He nodded towards the bath. This was insane.

"Turn around then."

"Hm?"

"Eyes front, Seb. I'm not stripping in front of you."

He chuckled, nodding. "As you say, beautiful." He turned around, leaning his shoulder against the door frame. I turned around to face the opposite direction, feeling foolish as a girl. I could see the shape of him, hazy in the steamed-up mirror, as I slid my shorts off and folded my underwear inside them. The top was next, bra undone and slid within as well, and I shed my socks quickly. He hadn't moved from his spot, his shoulders still front and centre, and if I lingered in my looking, it was purely to be sure he wasn't peaking on me.

I got into the water, sinking down quicker than I usually would, so I was covered. "You're good."

He turned around, giving me a lazy smile as he came closer. "You gonna turn around for me to see your back, or am I checking these by touch?"

I rolled my eyes at him, sinking lower to turn on my hip. There were enough bubbles to keep everything modest, as he'd said, but my skin was tingling with something other than them popping when I rose again. "Better?"

"Much." He knelt beside the bath, running his fingers along my slick shoulders. "There's a fair number of scratches. Only one looks deep, right here." He ran his nail underneath a cut a little above my shoulder blade and a thrill of pain spiked out, but it was no worse than the bump on my head.

I huffed a shallow laugh. "Right, so no backless dress, either. We're really limiting Marie's options here."

"Why were you out in the woods, Kat?"

I looked over my shoulder at him. "Jogging. I had bad dreams last night, I thought getting out would help. Felt nice to be in the woods again. I didn't get out there much before we left."

"You could have come and cuddled me."

I raised my brows at him, resisting the urge to splash water over the lip of the bath. "I'm sure you would've loved that."

"I would." I couldn't tell what that look meant, all soft and golden as honey, but I refused to take him on.

"Alright. Next time I wake up screaming, I'll come find you."

"You won't have to, after tomorrow. We'll be sharing the bed."

That was enough to put a bucket of cold water over any warm thoughts I might be having. The wedding night. That was…. Inevitable. Yes. "Of course. I bet you hog all the covers." It was a weak line, and I knew it.

He took mercy on me, shaking his head. "I'll try my best not to. Anyway, there'll be some turning happening before we even get to that stage, so you'll have time to steal them to your side."

I nodded, humming at the idea. "It'll be okay that I can't?"

"Yes, that's fine. We can talk about that more with the family."

"Sounds good." I swallowed, my tongue heavy with the questions I wanted to ask. While in the bath. This was the stupidest thing I'd done outside of going jogging.

"Now, if you want, I'll sit by the window so you can do what you need to, and I'll tell you about the Campbells. Sound alright?"

"Yeah, sounds good." I nodded, trying to tug a smile up, and he gave me one in return.

"Good. But don't take too long. Your hair'll go frizzy with the humidity." Seb stood up, moving to the window. The creak of him opening it a crack was a welcome break in the discussion, enough to let my shoulders sink down a little.

"How do you remember that?"

"I remember the noises you made while your mum brushed it out."

I laughed, the memory swooping in my chest like a swallow in the spring. "She hated combing my hair out."

"Only as much as any parent does. I doubt Marie was much better for our mother."

I shook my head, turning over again once he was "She had lovely hair as a kid. It was like gold."

"Still is." The pride in his voice was wonderful, a warmth all his own. It was nice to think of him taking care of her, even with everything now on his plate.

"I'm looking forward to seeing her again. Now, you were going to tell me about the new wolves?"

"The Campbells, yes. They are in a predicament. Their old leader died about a year ago, give or take, in a fight over territory. Human territory."

"Crime?" I asked.

"Yes."

"Nasty."

Seb tutted. "Such is the life. We've been shifting away from anything other than muscle and enforcement for a while, but other packs have not. It leads to issues."

"So someone killed him, and what?"

"It caused a schism. About a third of the pack went off, out of the area, and they've not made the numbers back yet."

"So the leader, Will, is looking to challenge you, but with fewer men?"

"They want to get mates from the pack."

"Oh, shit. No."

"No?" I could hear the eyebrow being raised even if I was stubbornly not looking at him.

"Not if they have guys like Josh in there. He'd be terrible with someone from here."

"Glad we agree there, then." There was a smile in his words, at least. "He was looking to have some of the young women pair up. Not to fold in, like Victor did, but to take them off and build up numbers."

"Right. I think that's a terrible idea." I took the loofa up, scrubbing my skin as quietly as I could.

"My father agreed. It's caused some contention."

"Have they tried to grab anyone?"

"Not yet, but you're thinking along the right lines. I think he'll escalate as he gets angrier."

"So the wedding is a show of power as well as getting things done."

"Of sorts, yes. We've had no active fights, but given they're clearly keeping eyes on us, I expect there's a plan for something like that."

"What if they try to kill you?" I didn't look at him as I asked, but I heard the intake of breath. Of course I was going to ask about it. He hadn't remembered me that well if he thought I'd miss that detail.

"Challenging me directly would be foolish."

"You have a big event coming up. We are the big event. If I was looking for an excuse to cause a scene, I'd do it then."

He hummed, not a no, but clearly not agreeing. "That would be… unbecoming."

"So is scaring little girls, no?"

"You're hardly little."

"I meant Annabelle, you obtuse sod." I almost threw the loofa at him.

"Sorry." He wasn't, I could tell from his voice. "You're right that Josh's behaviour was irregular. I am still willing to have him barred from the event."

"No, it's fine. We'll get more out of showing them up."

"We?"

"I am 'team us' for the foreseeable future, since I don't want to get stabbed. Speaking of which, I presume someone had checked that Josh and Will didn't harm your dad?"

"Yes. Part of why I waited to come and get you was in case that was it. They were working, as was most of their pack, at a concert. I can't see them sending an underling to get him. Or an underling succeeding, frankly."

"Don't discount the underdog. I agree though. I can't see your dad falling for that. So, do we think they'll do something at the wedding?"

"You seem to."

"Maybe I have a low opinion of men who try to choke me."

“Maybe.” He sounded closer, and when I turned to look, he was almost beside the bath. “I’ll go get you a towel. I can see Marie checking the windows at her house. She’s going to be over soon if we don’t go there.”

“There and then introductions?”

“Yes. I want my mother to be there when you meet everyone. She’s been throwing herself into preparations and looking after the kids, but they should see her in her position.”

“No problem. Toss a towel in and I’ll get dressed.”

“I’m patching you up before we go.”

“Whatever you say.”

CHAPTER 12

"Kitty-Kat!" The weight of Marie thumping into a hug was enough to knock the air out of me and my feet back a few steps, but I wrapped my arms around her as I got myself stable.

"Hey you," I said. She squeezed me tight, enough that I groaned at the protest from my ribs, and she laughed with the same loud bark of noise that she had when we were younger.

"Daniel told me you got attacked. What happened?" She pulled away, turning me in her hold so she could check me over. "You look pale."

"I've always been pale, Marie." I laughed, patting one of her hands. The touch of skin on skin brought a rush of the scent of blood and peaches, a telltale sign of something not yet showing underneath her chic black shirt. "Wait, are you?"

"Shh!" She put a finger to her lips, glancing about. We were standing on her porch, Seb still speaking to Daniel behind us, so it was not as if anyone could overhear the question. "Come in and speak."

She dragged me into their house, through the open living room and into a large kitchen before she let go of my wrist. Her face was torn, half a smile up as she twisted her hands together.

“Are you okay?” I asked.

She nodded, closing the door. “Yes! Yes I am, I mean.” She patted her stomach, lips pinching. “It’s great news! Only it’s not, because of what happened with dad, and we had the mourning period, and you can’t tell people *this* when that’s going on, and it’s only four months so we’re nervous and, oh, Kat.”

Her face screwed up like she might cry, and I ushered her into a hug again, stroking the back of her head. “I’m delighted for you. I won’t say anything at all. Does Seb know?”

She shook her head frantically. “No, no one but me and Daniel, and our mother. She noticed it really early. But you can’t say anything until at least three months, just in case. Wolf pregnancies can be unpredictable. And then we were trying to figure out how to tell people properly. Then dad died.” She was turning red from the rush of speaking.

“That’s alright, no stress. I won’t know about it until I’m told. I’ll even act surprised. That’s so lovely for you.”

“It’ll have to be after the wedding when we announced it. We’d be stealing your thunder otherwise.”

I pulled back to look at her, face flushed but with no tears, thankfully. “Don’t be silly, I wouldn’t be angry about that.”

"You might not be, but Seb would be. The wedding's important to him. And to the pack."

"I know." I nodded, glancing behind us to the kitchen. It was a friendly space, well-lit from a pair of long windows that looked across to the woods. "Come on, let's get the coffee on so they don't think anything's up."

She nodded, taking my hands in hers and giving a little squeeze. "I'm so glad you're back, Kat. I was so worried, after what happened with dad, and those bastards sneaking around in the woods."

"Yeah, I met an absolute creep called Josh. That wasn't fun."

"Daniel said, I'm so sorry."

"Don't fret, it's fine." Maybe best not to mention the man with a knife. I nudged our shoulders together, so we were nearly standing beside each other, facing into the kitchen. "Is he always like that?"

"Josh? Ugh, yes, he's gross. I don't mind him being a bit sleezy, lots of the guys are coming up. They get it out of their system, but he's not just being an idiot. He really thinks like that. And they want to move in on some of our girls! Not a chance. I'll chop their bits off first." She shook her head with a finality, brows tight and low. Unmanning them might not be the best negotiation tactic, but she was certainly her father's daughter.

I giggled, taking cups from the first set I found in a cupboard. They didn't match but could look almost cohesive at a glance. It would do. "Are we making coffee for your mother as well?"

"Yes, please, if you grab five cups, that would be good."

"No problem." I set the five out, digging into the fridge for milk.

"I'll see where the guys are, two seconds." She bustled out of the kitchen and I smiled to myself as the coffee machine bubbled away. This was domestic, and not at all like my mornings usually were, but there was a lingering warmth from when Marie had hugged me. It was nice. Almost like I could slot back in to where things had been before.

As I was digging through lower cupboards for sugar, the door opened again, and turning I saw Gillian, their mother, stood in one of the side doors. She was beautiful as ever, green eyes rather than Seb's hazel, but the same regal looking beauty as Marie: high cheekbones, a proud jut to her lower lip. She stood stiff, shoulders tense, and I smiled at her to lessen the shock.

"Hello, Gillian. Marie's just chasing the other two in. I'm sorry to hear of all your troubles."

"Thank you." She closed her eyes briefly, nodding her head. "It is good to see you again, Kathryn."

"And you. I wish it was on better terms."

"As do I." She didn't step closer yet.

"How do you take your coffee?"

"Does Bastian know what you are?" The question hit me like a slap, enough to make me drop the bag I'd picked up. I caught it before it exploded over the counter, setting it down as I looked up at her again. Just for a second, I was small again, and she was the grownup and I was in trouble, but it didn't last long.

My throat was dry, and I swallowed before I answered. "He knows I'm not trained. That I have fire, like my father, but nothing else."

"That's not what I mean."

I sighed, smile dropping. Here we go. "I know. Have you told him?"

"No."

"Then no. I didn't until my mother was dying. She lied as long as she could, thinking it was a mercy." I turned away, spooning sugar into two cups as I knew I took it, and Bastian would.

"He should know."

"Why? I won't be doing anything." I refused to turn and lash out at her, despite the creak at my jaw where it clenched. Dead men's plans back to haunt me again. A wickedness I hadn't asked for.

"You're a weapon, Kathryn. Do you know how to be that safely?"

"Does a vegetable knife know it can cut meat?" I asked, shaking my head. "It doesn't matter what the designs were, it's a knife either way. Sharpen it the right way and everyone bleeds. Friend or foe." I swallowed again, shifting the pain in my throat. "My fire is instinctual. I'll do my best to keep that safe for everyone, but if people insist on attacking me, it will flare up."

"You know that's not what I mean."

"Say it plainly then, Gillian." I forced my shoulders down, turning and tilting my chin at her. "Tell me what you mean, because you probably know more about it than I do."

"It would be better for you not to marry him if you would cause him harm."

"Better I get stabbed by someone in my home?" I tugged the edge of my top, showing the dressing Seb had placed there. "Better I die like John did?"

She flinched at the comment, and shame burned as hot as my impotent anger. "There isn't only you to think about. The pack. How will you have children?"

I blinked at her, not following. "The usual way, I imagine."

"Wolf pregnancies are difficult for humans. It would kill a normal human. Untrained, you could haemorrhage out and take the baby too. That's more pain than anyone should have to suffer."

"Especially after he's lost his dad so soon, too. I am sorry, for your loss. John deserved better."

"Thank you. He did." She sniffed, and I hated myself all over again. "I take one sugar, please. We should discuss this matter with more care. And with Bastian."

I didn't speak while I made her coffee, taking the cup and milk over to the counter. "Will you tell him?"

She stared at me for a long beat. "No. That should be you."

"We're due to marry tomorrow. Doesn't give me much time. And I am loath to get killed because of pack politics, to be honest."

She took the cup, and the smile she had was equal parts pain and patience. "I know. Choose how you wish to go ahead. It would be reasonable for you to want protection until we have solved the killing and then seek your own life again. I'm furious that we don't have more justice there yet. But I won't forgive you if you harm my son."

"I understand. I don't think my mother ever forgave any of you."

Gillian stilled, cup partway to her mouth. She set it down and looked at me like I was a child again, an understanding that I didn't *want.* I felt the gap between us like a river to be crossed. "No, I imagine not. I am sorry about that. I missed Sophie very much when you both left. Your mother was a good woman. Strong."

"I think, sometimes, she missed you. We didn't talk much about it, and when she was sick, it became less of a focus. But I think she did."

"Thank you. That's a kind thing to say. We should take the cups through."

"Sure." I walked back over to the counter, pouring the rest of the coffee. "I know Marie's news, by the way."

"You could tell?"

"Peaches and blood. I always get that scent when someone's expecting. Comes with the magic. I presume."

"How wonderful for you to know. We haven't told anyone. John didn't even know." There was a smile in her voice, but it still sounded far off. Grief was a pointed thing.

"I'm sorry to hear that." I meant it, trite as it would sound. "It would have been nice for him to know. I'll keep quiet."

"Thank you. I'll go see where they are, if you can carry the cups?"

"Of course. I waited enough tables to manage four cups."

"Thank you." She came close beside me, setting a hand on my arm, by the elbow. "I am truly glad to have you back, Kathryn. I thought of you often."

I couldn't help the bite in my question. "Because you missed me or because you were worried I'd find out?"

"Both." She paused, tilting her head a little, as if considering. "Honestly, both. I would be happy to have you with us now, too. If it's safe."

"Thank you." I looked away, huffing a sigh to settle my breathing. "It will be nice to be here a while, at least."

"We'll need to—"

The kitchen door crashed open, the bulk of Daniel spilling through it. "Kat, we need you in here."

"Are you alright?" I set the cups down, rushing over to him.

"Yeah, yeah I'm fine, but uh. Well. Come through." He nodded back through the door and I went after him, Gillian close behind us.

Seb and Marie were standing in the living room, grim faced and staring at a phone. My phone. I patted my pockets and found it wasn't there.

"What's going on?" I asked. "Why do you have my phone?"

"It must have fallen out when I hugged you. Seb brought it in," Marie said. She had her arms wrapped around herself, and Daniel crossed to her, pecking a kiss to her hair.

"Kat, do you know an Elaine Wilson?" Seb asked, handing me the phone back.

"Yeah, why?"

"She just called you. Well, had called you about seventeen times, I saw the latest call coming in and answered it."

"Is she okay?" Mrs Wilson would never call like that unless there was a problem.

"Someone broke into your shop last night. They tried to start a fire. She seems to be fine. I don't think it did more than smoke damage, but she was worried sick about you. You should call her. I don't think she trusted me much." Seb gave a sheepish grin, shrugging. "She has no reason to, of course."

"A fire?" My brain latched onto the word, all my books and pages stained black or charred.

"It might be to do with the other event from last night," Seb said.

"They could have killed her. She lives alone in that flat, other than her birds."

"Call her and we can speak about it once you know she's alright." Seb rubbed the back of my hand, brows down low.

"You can use the kitchen. We'll stay in here," Marie said. "I'll get the coffees and clear out."

"Right. Yeah, sure." I nodded, grip on the phone tight. "We can do that."

CHAPTER 13

"Mrs Wilson?" I spoke as soon as the call connected, breathless to know she was alright.

"Kat, where on earth are you?"

I sighed, could have sobbed, and the stern answer. She was fine. She wouldn't be giving me a hard time if she was hurt. "I had to stay overnight somewhere last night. There was a problem at my house. Are you okay?"

"More smoked than I used to be. I don't think Coconut has ever been so scared."

The parrot was alright then too, good. I'd never forgive myself if that bird had been killed. "I'm so sorry, Mrs Wilson. Did you call the police?"

"Of course! And the insurance. Which you might want to do too, honey. We got the fire out, but they kicked your window in like a horse was at it, and the bits they burned are pretty black. There's also water damage from when we were putting it out."

"That's okay, property damage is much better than people damage. I was more worried about you and the girlies." I sank against the counter, my back to the edge as I half folded into myself. They were okay.

"Well, you might have to bring some banana chips before they forgive you, but we're fine. Who was that young 'un who answered your phone, by the way?"

"Hm?"

"That man. A very polite thing, he was."

"Oh, that's Bastian. He's who I was staying with last night."

"Oh?" The purr in her voice was enough to send my cheeks hot again, and I could picture the arch of her eyebrow as if she were standing before me.

"He's an old friend. He let me stay over when I'd had a fright."

"Kathryn, honey, you don't have friends except the post office counter girl." I winced at the comment, unable to summon much rebuke other than a startled laugh. She wasn't wrong, but it stung in a morning of other pains.

"I, uh. I know him from before my mother got sick. Old friends that way. Not recent." Gods, that sounded pathetic. I twisted on my feet, turning to look out of the window in a vain attempt at distraction.

"Well, I might have been a touch sharp with him. I wasn't expecting no man to answer your phone. Especially not one you hadn't brought past me first."

That brought a smile up to my face, the fussy protective bustle of her usual morning routine showing, even on a call. "I'll be sure to bring him around so you can check him over. How about that?"

"That's more like it." I could picture her nodding and heard the caw of one bird agreeing. "Now you scurry your butt down here and get this checked out. The whole town will be worried about it."

"I'm a little way aways, but I'll get there as soon as I can. And I'll bring banana chips."

"That's my girl. You make sure you come up and see me when you get here, okay?"

"Yes, Mrs Wilson. You take care."

She hummed in approval, and I hung up the call. Setting the phone down, I took a step back so I could fold my arms onto the counter and rest my head against them, straighten my spine out flat until it stretched the long muscles at the back of my legs.

It shouldn't be a surprise there had been a break in. Someone had been in my home. Armed. Someone had hurt me. It twisted in my gut, though, that my little shop was targeted too. All the parts of me that were normal, and good, being picked apart and hurt by someone I didn't even know.

"Kat?" Seb's voice sounded at the door, and I stood up, wiping my face quickly.

"Hey, yeah, I'm still here."

He stepped into the kitchen, closing the door. His face was tight, pinched like it had been in my kitchen the night before, and he rested his back on the wood. "Are you alright?"

"Yes. Mrs Wilson sounded well, despite the fire. I think she'll be giving me hell for a few days, but we knew that was a risk of me running off with you."

Seb stepped closer, his hands up as if in mock surrender. "Am I to be introduced as the ruffian stealing you away?"

"I said you were an old friend. To which she said I didn't have any friends, other than Ellie, at the post office. Which might be truer than I like to admit, honestly."

He smiled and did his best to hide a chuckle. "She sounds quite fearsome."

"She's a great lady. Retired, living off a pension, helps me out with parcels." I wrapped my arms around myself, shaking my head. "She shouldn't be getting frightened off by attempted arson."

"I'll send some guys over to secure the place."

"I'll need to go too. There's insurance to sort out, and I'll need to check for damage."

Seb shook his head. "If there's been an attack there too, they could be trying to draw you out."

"Do you even hear yourself? I'm not some spy, Seb. I own a shop. If they're trying to draw someone out, it'll be you, surely?"

"They may try to hurt you to get to me." He stepped closer, almost enough to touch me but holding back.

"Then come along as well and they can attack you instead."

He tilted his head to one side, as if he were considering it. "That could work. Would mean we'd need to take separate cars, one for us and one for the men."

I covered my face with my hands. "Seriously?"

"You need a dress. I had planned on my mother and Marie going out with you to do that, but maybe it would be better if I came instead."

"That's bad luck, you seeing me in the dress," I said from behind my hands.

"Worse luck than getting cut open?"

"It's a shame my fire doesn't work on you. I'd quite like to set you alight."

He laughed, the same loud sound as Marie, stepping in to tug me into a hug. "I bet you'd feel bad afterwards."

"Not convinced I would." I let my head rest on his shoulder. Much too familiar, of course, but it looked good. And it felt nice, silly as that was. He was solid.

"Who'd drive you back to the shop if you did?"

"I bet Daniel would, if I said I'd give him some free books."

"Bribery already, hm?" Seb chuckled into my hair, shaking his head. "You really are fitting straight in."

"Just like riding a bike." I hadn't meant it to sound so petulant, so bitter, but my mind felt as black as the soot damage I was yet to see.

"I know this isn't easy, Kat. I'm sorry to sound flippant. But I'd rather they attacked your shop than get you. And I don't want you to go risking yourself because you feel responsible."

"I don't feel responsible." It was a lie that tasted bad on my tongue. He pulled back, eyebrows raised. "Not for the attack. I feel… worried that innocent people are going to get hurt. I don't want that. And I don't want my life to be crumpled up because I'm with you."

"I know, I know." He nodded, leant in close for the hug for a second longer. "It won't be. We'll be wed tomorrow, and we can discuss what to do next after that. Today, let's get on with the meeting and then we can look at your shop, then go shopping. I'll take you myself."

I pulled back to look at him. "Just us?"

"Yes. Why?"

"I don't know how good your fashion sense is. I mean, you suit the leather jacket, but I'm not exactly going for the biker bride look." The joke felt as weak as the smile that accompanied it, but he laughed.

"I'll let you take the lead, then. And screw the idea of bad luck, we make our own here."

I nodded to him, taking a deep breath and holding it until I pushed off the counter to follow him into the living room.

Daniel, Marie, and Gillian were standing together in a little huddle, far off from the door, and they all turned to face us when the door opened.

"Is everything okay?" Marie asked.

"My upstairs neighbour isn't hurt, and neither are her birds, so that's good. I'm going to have to take them some treats to make up for the worry, but we should be fine. I'll need to go to the shop too. Get it secured."

"Fred and I can do that." Daniel looked between Seb and I. "He's great with securing places."

"We'll go over after the meeting. You and Fred in one car, me and Kat in another. I want to take her dress shopping afterwards."

"I thought we were doing that?" Marie pushed past Daniel to poke at Seb, nose wrinkled in anger.

"You were, until someone tried to play pyro with her shop. I'm not risking all the women I love at once. You can still be in charge of helping her get ready, but I don't want you three all out together."

"Bastian's right, sweetheart." Gillian stepped forward, an arm going around Marie's shoulders. "If there's still attacks going on, we should all be cautious. And it's a marvellous chance for these two to catch up some more. Make joint choices." Gillian caught my eye, and I brought up a bright smile.

"Exactly. I can show you the dress when we get back, and we can talk about the ceremony. We don't have too long left, so better we split the tasks."

"It sounds like it's already decided, then." Marie crossed her arms, near rolling her eyes when Gillian pressed a kiss to her hair. "He has terrible taste, so you know, so don't let him choose."

"Hey!" Seb shook his head.

I laughed, nudging my shoulder into his. "I won't. Anyway, he's going to be carrying the bags, so I can always run off and switch it out."

"That's more like it." Marie grabbed my hands again. "I mean it though, you choose. This is your day, too."

"You make it sound so grim. She's not going to the gallows, Marie." Daniel slid an arm around her shoulders, nuzzling her hair. It sent a pang through my chest, the act so soft, an intimacy that it seemed wrong to watch. I glanced at Seb, the smile on his face just as fond and open. My heart ached, a little, at the softness there.

"Exactly. This is a joyful event. A nice way for us all to move forward, despite the other things happened." Gillian said. "Come on, people will be keen to meet Kathryn."

"Now?" I asked.

"Yes. It's going to have to be cut short with this extra trip, but we can show face and mingle, then head off." Seb took my arm in his, our elbows together like a proper couple, and led me towards the door. "We'd usually have a bit more ceremony about it, but given what happened this morning, I'd rather keep it close."

"Alright. That's fine for me." This was all false anyway. Best put on a good show.

Seb opened the door and instead of the empty dirt square of earlier, when we had crossed over from the bigger house, we were met by a scrum of bodies: easily fifty people milling around with coffee and what I thought could be donuts as someone shifted around to look at us. I spotted a couple of tables set up, dotted with large urns of coffee and open snack boxes. I couldn't help my smile, or the growl my stomach gave, and I slapped a hand to it in embarrassment.

"Good morning!" Seb shouted, walking us down Marie's porch steps and into the throng of people. "I'm glad to see so many of you here. With the wedding night fast approaching, I wanted to take this opportunity to present my mate to you all." His hand slid closer to entwine our fingers, holding them up so everyone could see our joined hands. The crowd burst into claps, some of the young men I half recognised whistling loudly between their fingers. My face burned at the sudden reaction, but I smiled, giving a small wave with my free hand.

"Some of you already know Kathryn, from her time with the pack previously, and for some of you, this will be your first time meeting her. She is an independent witch, having lived her own life before re-joining us. That will continue after the marriage as well. I would that we had more time to speak to everyone, and share the good news, but my darling wife requires a wedding dress and I would be remiss in not ensuring she gets the best ahead of the celebration tomorrow."

"That's bad luck!" shouted someone, one of the young women.

"We make our own luck in the Weir Pack!" Seb shouted back. Another cheer went up, then more clapping, and I jolted as Marie came up behind us and slid her arm around my waist.

"You're doing great," she whispered.

"Thanks."

"Make sure he doesn't pick the dress."

"Marie!" Gillian hissed, coming to stand beside her daughter. We were a united front, the line of family at the head of the pack for everyone to see, and I kept my smile up as I looked around at the faces staring back at us. I knew some of them. Not a lot. Not enough.

Marie's pout was clear in her voice. "You know I'm right."

Once the shouts and claps had died off, Sebastian continued, "We will be here for the next few minutes while we make arrangements, so if you want to come and speak, please do. It will be good for everyone to catch up."

"Get ready for it," Marie said.

"Hm?"

"The girls are dying to meet you." She nodded to a gaggle of young girls - pushing and pulling each other like the line of a tide - who looked ready to run forward.

"Why?" I asked out the side of my mouth.

"Because you're the famous witch Seb is in love with. Everyone knows stories about you."

My heart sank at every part of that sentence, and then they were coming towards me before I could escape.

CHAPTER 14

The girls landed in front of us, nodding to Marie before their eyes turned to me. They were like a little line of blinking owls, tall enough to be getting into their changes but still soft at the edges, enormous eyes open and demanding. Annabelle stood to the far side, stealing glances at me before looking away again. They must all be eleven or twelve, if that, pushing through the awkward stage and into their own.

"Say hello," Marie prompted.

"I'm Karin," the one at the front said. "My cousin Daniel says you're going to let us look at your website." She was tall, with curly hair that fuzzed around her like a dark halo.

"Daniel said you might help me with it. It's a bit old."

"Karin's good at that. I help with the graphics." The next in line spoke up, nudging Karin. "I'm Amy." Amy was shorter, with the russet brown hair of some of the other families, a darker blonde showing through strong in her long braid.

"Nice to meet the both of you." I smiled at them, glancing at the others. "Did you want to talk to me about the website? I can meet up with you to talk about that.

It' something for when you have downtime. No pressure."

"Is it true you attacked a wolf?" the one next to Annabelle blurted out, all in a rush like she'd been keeping it in. She was gangly tall, all the long bones coming in first, with wicked red hair that blazed in the sunlight. Bound to be beautiful when she grew into it.

"Harper!" The squeak came from Marie, her brows up in a threat that was just like Gillian when we were younger.

Harper pouted; hands shoved into the pockets of her shorts. "Annabelle said Kat saved her. I bet she was really cool."

"Annabelle was very brave," I said, leaning in like I was sharing a secret. "She went and got help. Help is better than fighting on your own." They would know that, of course, a gaggle of girls all together like this. But there was no harm in telling them that, especially when Annabelle might still be upset.

"You fought, though," Karin said, pointing to my chest. "Cousin Daniel said Seb had to patch you up."

I blanked for a second, unsure how good the truth would be to share. Maybe a half-truth. They couldn't see the dressing through this top. "Of course, I did. I didn't come up with the pack without knowing how to tussle a bit. You never let them have an inch, if you can help it. That's why we get help. That guy was lucky I didn't get something really special out for him, threatening one of you girls."

"Like what?" Harper pushed closer, dragging Annabelle with her.

"I'm a witch, not a magician. I don't just do tricks." I winked at them, shaking my head. "Maybe I'll show you after the wedding. Until then, I'm sure everyone's much too busy to put out a fire."

"You can make fire?" Harper was clearly the magic fan. Annabelle looked interested too, peering at me with those big doe eyes.

"Does it hurt?" Amy asked. She'd wrapped one arm around Karin's, squeezing tight onto it.

"Hopefully, you'll never have to find out. I'm sure everyone will work hard to keep you safe without my magic. But, if there's something really scary, you can come find me. I'll show whatever it is there's a lot more to fear when they go against us."

They giggled, pushing together before Marie stepped in. "Right, you lot, off with you. Other people will want to speak to Kat."

"Can we call you Kat?" Annabelle asked. Her voice was stronger now, clearer than it was in the woods, and it was a rush of relief to hear her sounding like the others rather than the wavering upset.

"Yes, that's what lots of people call me."

"After tomorrow, it should be Mrs Weir," Karin said.

I laughed, a little thrill of anxiety sparking in my chest. "That's my formal name. You don't call Seb Mr Weir, do you?"

"Not even when they should," Marie said. She was so fond, despite the low draw of her brows. "Now go, there's only a few donuts left."

Annabelle tugged on Harper's arm and they turned, all four of them tumbling off like birds out to sea.

"They're cute," I said.

Marie laughed. "They're menaces. Worse than the boys, that lot."

"Why?"

"Because the boys are daft until they hit thirteen. Those girls are sharp."

I nudged her elbow. "Good thing they're here with us then. We'll have a right little task force."

Marie smiled, her hand resting over her stomach just longer than it should have. "I hope so."

"Just you watch. I bet they'll be great at the wedding, too."

"A wedding that we need to get you a dress for. You should get Seb on that."

"Want me to send you pictures of the options?" I waggled my phone at her.

"Oh, yes! Here." She grabbed my phone, typing her number in. "Send me as many as you can. I'll keep our mother occupied, but I want to see what you pick."

"Alright, no problem." I gave her a quick half hug, unsure if it was for show or if I meant it. It didn't matter either way. If there were eyes on us, it looked like it should and that was enough. "Come on, introduce me to folk before we have to go deal with paperwork."

~

"How are you feeling?" Seb asked. We were driving back down the same road as last night, the forest still a dark blur beside us. Sunlight peaked through the tall tips, striping the road with shadow and light which we slid through like a fish under ice.

"I'm fine." I looked over at him, sat easily in the driver's seat.

"Your throat okay?"

"Sore, but nothing a mint won't help with."

"Hm." His lips pinched together before he poked a button on the console. A little compartment opened down low, near the gearstick. "There are some mints in there."

I laughed, reaching in to find a folded packet. "Thanks. You really are prepared for everything."

"I drive a lot. Helps."

I took a mint out for me and him, folding the packet up and putting it away again. The compartment shut automatically. "Are you alright?" I asked. I held the mint up to his lips, and he opened them, accepting the little white disk.

"Why do you ask?"

"I doubt you're taking me dress shopping because you have strong opinions on necklines and lace." I took my mint on my tongue, the heat of it blossoming like toothpaste. It was strong enough to make the air in my nostrils heat a little, but when that passed, there was a pleasant sweetness.

He huffed, shaking his head. "I want to be involved. It's our wedding. I will confess, I am worried though. The attack at your house is one thing, but to attack your shop the same night? That's either idiotic or an attempt at provocation and I lean to the latter."

"Moreso than that in the woods?"

"We'll still have to deal with that. They don't know who you are, or at least they didn't until the rough introduction earlier."

The words struck me like a bell, snagging around like a tangle of seaweed. "How do you mean?"

"It's been known that I'm promised. That was never in doubt, but outside of the pack, we haven't openly disclosed who you are."

"So, why did you come to get me?"

He sighed, shoulders hunching for a moment. "I suspected your details had got out. My father kept tabs on you, you know that. That's how I came to find you."

"Yes."

"Give the irregularities of how he died, I worried your details had been disclosed too."

"Why?"

"His office was wrecked. I've not told anyone but the core families, for obvious reasons, but there's a real risk they grabbed his old records. Jobs, personal details, your information, more than that even."

"I'm going to state the obvious thing."

"Go on."

"Are you sure it wasn't one of the pack?" He turned to look at me, and my gut twisted as he held my gaze. "Seb, road!"

"It's fine." He looked back. The car had indeed been fine. He wasn't drifting, but my heart was up in my throat. "Why would you say that?"

"John wasn't an idiot. I might not have liked him at times, but he was careful. I can't imagine him letting someone in his office to do that."

"He was out in the woods when he died."

"Yeah, you said."

He was working his jaw, chewing his words before he said them. "He wasn't warm when I found him."

"Sorry, Seb."

"It means it had been a while." I hummed a yes, unsure where this was going. "Long enough for someone to make it back and wreck the place."

"You already thought it?"

"I wouldn't say that. I haven't."

"But it's been in your head."

"I can't think someone in the pack would. I can't." He slapped the steering wheel, the sound loud as a clap of thunder in the small space, and I flinched into the door. My seatbelt was on, it was fine, we were safe, but I saw the way his eyes flashed with hurt when he looked over. "I'm sorry."

"It's alright." My voice was much too small, a silly measure of leftover fear. I didn't need to be afraid of Seb. I knew that. The last day or so had left me with an excess of adrenaline, though, and it pulled my nerves as tight as I could stomach. "I'm alright."

He frowned, eyes back to the road. "I shouldn't be making you scared."

"Everything is making me scared. You're not special. Knifes and wolves and arson, oh my. Worst thing I had to worry about before was a delivery guy being weird."

"Bet not many of them tried that with you."

"Not more than once."

He laughed, but it was a push of air, barely there. "I understand why you would ask the question. It's natural. I don't think someone in the pack would, but you've been away. Of course, you would see things that way."

"There are a lot of kids," I said, scrambling for something else to talk about. "In the pack, I mean. I saw more than I expected."

"We've changed how we do certain things."

"Oh?"

"It was Marie's idea, originally, but my dad took it and ran with it. Any recent turns get invited to live with us now."

"I don't follow."

"If anyone's been bitten, and we find them, we offer them a place. They have to do a few moons with us before the move permanently, so we know they're safe and there's nothing negative about the change, but yeah. It's brought a lot of fresh blood in to us."

"No wonder."

"And we have an adoption rule. If any of the men are killed on jobs, we adopt their kids into the pack. Human or wolf, but it's mostly been wolves."

"You claim them?"

"It's a negotiated thing. We don't snatch kids. But, yes. They have a place with us, even if the wolf parent isn't here anymore. The family isn't only those who run under the moon."

"Right."

I sat back in my seat, mulling that over. On the one hand, it was more job security than anything else I'd heard of. You knew they would look after your family. While it was a bit mobster, the pack was not a grim group, and any kids would be taken care of. Despite some of their activities. On the other, it made my heart ache at the idea of a family like that. The things I had missed when my mother and I ran off from them and into the wall of effort we'd faced after we left.

It would never have been safe. I knew that, now, understood why she'd run. But the gap in what could have been was huge, and I felt cold like a north wind at the thought of the difference. Could I have loved Seb, knocking together like that? Could it have been an actual marriage between us? I looked over at him, eyes carefully on the road. He was handsome, that was never a doubt, and he was fierce in the way he planned to look after everyone. There was a lot to like in that.

"You okay?" His voice was low, soft like he'd been after I got cut last night.

"Yeah."

"You've gone quiet on me, Kat."

"Just thinking."

"Good thing one of us does."

I snorted, shaking my head at him. "Shut up with that. You graduated. I missed my night school graduation for a spare shirt."

"You're right." He sighed, deep as a well. "I wish I'd come and told you then. Made that connection, then."

"I'd probably have been horrible to you."

"Yeah?"

"I was horrible to your dad. And Victor. At least he seems to have forgiven me."

"He's looking forward to the ceremony."

"Really?"

"He's the official, since my father isn't here. As my father's second, it falls to him instead. One last thing for my father, as a mark of respect."

"That's nice. Sweet that it's someone whose known us both, too. I'm glad about that."

"Good, I'm happy that's okay with you."

I smiled over at him, patting his hand. "Don't fret so much. We're doing this for the pack and it'll work out. You can find yourself a proper person once things aren't so crazy. It's like a test run. I don't mind being your test run."

"No?"

"No, course not. It's nice, because it's you." I was surprised to find that I meant it.

"You're gonna kill me saying things like that."

"Oh, hush." I laughed at him, sitting up now we were approaching the town. "Mrs Wilson will give you a hard enough time. What's the story going to be?"

"Tell her the truth?"

"That you're a werewolf heavy-man? Nix, she'll toss holy water at you. Maybe salt too."

He barked a laugh, pulling us up to the curb. "Maybe just fiancé?"

"Might still get you the salt."

"I'll risk it. Come on."

CHAPTER 15

Daniel and Fred joined us in evaluating the mess that was the front of my shop. The long bay window had been kicked in, which was as Mrs Wilson had said, and the door had been bust open, presumably from when the fire was being put out.

I looked at the now crooked handle, broken from being forced. I'd only locked up last night.

"Got security?" Daniel asked.

"Yeah, cameras on both doors and some inside. They're not huge, but they cover the blind spots."

"I suppose it's totally green to assume this was someone going for the cash register?" Fred asked. He was new - I didn't know him from growing up with them – but he was ages with the rest of us. His skin was suntan brown, with dark hair that he slicked down into an immaculate swoop at the front. He'd do well on the doors somewhere, an easy strength in the way he shifted his shoulders, even if he was only about height with me.

"I've not had that in the last five years. I don't think people expect scores of cash in the till. Not as much stuff to steal like in a jeweller."

Seb shook his head, poking some of the hanging glass out so it fell inside the shop. "We should check the damage inside. Why don't we look the place over and you get in touch with the insurers?"

"Sure, that works. I'll be in the office, and I'll probably need to take photos. Oh hell, I forgot to stop of banana chips."

"Want me to run get some? I saw a shop when we were driving in." Daniel thumbed towards the main part of the shopping street, which would be busy at this time of the morning.

"Yeah, grab some and get some water for everyone. Better to have some in the car." Seb nodded, taking his wallet out and passing Daniel a note. "Fred, you come with me."

"Sure thing." Fred nodded, stepping up behind Seb as he pushed the door open.

"Back shortly." Daniel jogged off down the street and I followed the other two inside.

It was a mess: they had started the fire in the far back corner, where there was a display of new books and craft card. At least it had been card, which didn't light as easily, that had maybe helped. The smoke damage arced out from there, black soot trailing about half the height of the wall and smoke marks blooming out like briar roses, snaking over in a tumbling mess. It reached out across the ceiling, and I thanked whatever was listening it hadn't caught properly. Poor Mrs Wilson.

“They didn’t have a clue what they were doing.” Fred whistled, and Seb elbowed him.

“He’s right. Card was a poor choice.” I looked away, wincing at the squelch of the carpet under my feet. That would need to be replaced.

“We should get some dehumidifiers, when the window’s closed up, get them taking the moisture out, so it doesn’t hurt the stock. The carpet’s fucked, ‘sucse my language.”

“I worked retail. You’re good, Fred,” I said.

“Don’t encourage him,” Seb called as they looked over the rest of the space.

My gut churned at the cost of all this: cleaning, new carpets, new stock. I’d accepted I might be less available for the shop over a couple of weeks, maybe restricted hours, but this meant the doors being properly shut. Businesses were always hungry things, that’s why insurance existed, but this was a lot of cash suddenly gone and no one here to earn it back.

I turned to go into the office, shucking my jacket off and dumping it onto the counter. The till was unchecked, still sat closed like I had abandoned it last night, not even shifted like they’d pulled at the cord. If they’d been looking for money, they could have picked it up and walked out with the damn thing.

Pushing the office door open, a wave of rot and sweet decay hit me, my stomach roiling at the concentrated stench. I gagged, covering my mouth with the back of my hand, and then a scream poured out as I saw what had caused it.

A streak of black fur was pinned into the wall, a heavy knife jabbed between its ribs to pin it in place. It was a cat, I could tell by the little points of its ears and the limp, hanging tail, and underneath someone had scrawled ‘seven lives left’.

“Kat!” Seb was at my side, yanking me back and away from the mess. “Fucking hell.”

“What is it, boss?” Fred was beside us, and Seb passed me over to him as I shook my head over and over. That couldn’t be real. It was. I knew the scent of death, but no. No one should have done that to something in my shop. It was a bookshop!

Fred reached forward and shut the door, turning me back into the main body of the shop. “You have a fridge in here, Kat?”

“In the stockroom. There’s a microwave and a fridge.”

“Got anything in there, like coke or carbonated water?” He had an arm around my shoulders, leading me away from the office and keeping me talking. I knew this treatment, recognised it from years ago, and half of me wanted to turn and find Seb, to make sure he wasn’t having to see that too.

“I keep a few cans of diet coke in there.”

“Right. I want you to get one, and keep it pressed against the back of your neck for at least a minute. Then hold it between your wrists, right here so it presses against the veins." He tapped the soft skin, the wiry blue blood vessels showing underneath. "You do that until one of us comes in, alright?"

"Is this a trick?"

"Cooling you down helps with the nausea. Running your wrists under cold water does similar, but it's good to have a drink too. The bubbles will help with feeling sick."

"Do you have first aid training?"

He laughed, bobbing his head to either side before he answered. "You could say so. I was a responder ambulance driver, before I got bit. Didn't want to risk blood exposure afterwards, too much risk to others, so I stopped. But it sticks with you."

"Good, means someone can keep an eye on Seb. He rushes into things."

"Didn't you beat on one of the rival wolves this morning?"

"Seb beat on him. I just smashed his nose."

"Ah, right, the couple that draws blood together stays together, of course." He had me through into the canteen, a little cupboard I'd repurposed. "You stay here and one of us will come back."

"Sure." I went to the fridge, plucking a can out and doing as he'd said. I knew I was crying, I could feel it on my face, but the shock had kept it a thin edge of upset, separate to the shaky rush of adrenaline that was slowly running out of me. Sat in the dim little space, I took deep breaths as I set the can against my skin, closing my eyes.

All I saw was the streak of black, the dull metal of the knife.

I opened them again, shaking the image away. Poor thing. My moping about it wouldn't help.

"Now, just who are you two? And where is Kathryn?" I quickly wiped my face at the sound of Mrs Wilson, dropping the can onto the top of the fridge so I could go find her.

Coming out, I saw her pointed a finger at Seb, who was doing his best impression of a hostage with his hands up in the air. She was a formidable lady, had worked as a nurse before changing into library work teaching literacy. Her shoulders were broad and when they went up towards her ears, as they did when she was outraged, she gave the impression of a fluffed-up hen, about to launch herself at something slithering nearby.

"I'm here, Mrs Wilson," I said. She turned to look at me, eyebrows going high as she took me in.

"I heard you screaming."

"I did. There's something pretty awful in the office."

"Worse than a fire?"

"Yes." I nodded, thankful Fred had closed the door. "It's nasty. Gave me a shock."

"Hm. And who are they?" She tilted her head towards the two men, side eyeing them openly.

"The blond is Bastian, and that's Fred behind him." I turned to them, holding a hand out towards the fuming lady. "This is Mrs Wilson, who has been a lifesaver for many of the years I've been here."

"Don't you be buttering me up. I know how useful I've been. What business do they have with you?"

"Bastian is the one you spoke to earlier. He answered my phone when I was making coffee."

"Your friend?"

"That's me. I'm Kat's fiancé. I thought it was only right I came to help assess the damage. They left a threat against her as well, so I'm glad I did."

"Hold on a moment, pretty boy." Mrs Wilson held a finger up again, pointing at him, before it turned to me. "Kathryn Mocur, did that boy just say fiancé?"

I nodded, stepping closer so I could catch Seb's fingers in mine. "We were an arranged marriage before my parents died. So I would be taken care of."

"He been paying for your shop?"

"No." I tried not to bristle at the question. She knew how hard I'd worked at this place.

She snorted. "Of course not. It's all been you. He's a bad fiancé then. Who is he really?"

"I truly am betrothed to Kat. We were promised together as teenagers. My family wanted her to have her own life before we wed, so she could support herself if anything happened to me."

"Awful forward thinking for a family that marries kids off." Her mouth pinched together, looking between the two men. "You know, an African Grey's beak has enough power to cut through a human's finger if it's agitated. And my Coconut hasn't settled down since the fire."

"Is she threatening to feed us to a bird?" Fred asked.

"Mrs Wilson, we don't need to do that." I went towards her, trying to smile without laughing. "One of Bastian's friends is off getting banana chips for Coco. He's a good man. If he'd made me shriek, I'd have been out of the door."

"He's the one I saw you getting into the car with last night. You didn't look too happy then."

I shouldn't have been surprised she was watching me from her window, but it startled the laugh out of me. "He didn't call ahead. I was surprised last night. I was upset at what's the office, and the fact my carpet's now probably able to grow watercress, nothing else."

"None of this has a wonderful sound to it, Kathryn. Your shop's been good all these years and now this? What had they done in the office?"

"You don't want to see it, ma'am," Fred said. "There's a threat to Kat's life and there's a dead animal."

"Oh, Kathryn. You come out of here right now. You can make your calls from my flat. I'm not having you around that sort of thing." She took my elbow, tugging me closer. "And if those men are threatening you, we can call the police as well."

"I'll bring your laptop up, if you want, love?" Seb called, nodding for me to go.

"Thanks."

I let Mrs Wilson usher me out, meeting Daniel at the door. He passed me the bag of chips, raising a brow at me. I pointed into the shop and he nodded, ducking his head to Mrs Wilson before he vanished. We started up her steps, swept clean as she did every day, and she turned to me before we went through the door.

"Kathryn, you are going to explain to me what is going on and why I shouldn't call the police as soon as we get into my living room."

"I thought the police would have been here already, with the fire," I said.

"Don't get cheeky with me, lady. I am this close to reporting you as kidnapped." She held up her forefinger and thumb, tutting at me.

"Mrs Wilson, do you think that I'd get into the car with him if that was the case?"

She poked my chest, and I swallowed the squeak of pain when she hit the dressing. "You would if he threatened me, or one of the others. You've got too big a heart in you."

I shivered at the comment, the feel of Josh's hands around my throat ghosting up for a moment. "You think too kindly of me."

"Hm. Not a whit of that. I'm going to make a cup of tea and you can start talking."

"Can I feed Coconut too?"

She opened the door, glancing back before she answered. "If she lets you. She's still very ruffled."

CHAPTER 16

The kettle whistled as I fed Coconut fat yellow chips, about the size of a squashed coin. Coconut was so called because, before she was rescued, she had plucked all her head feathers out and when they had grown back they were tufty, sticking out at odd angles. Like a coconut shack, Mrs Wilson had said, cooing at the bird like one would a new baby.

Coconut regarded me with her beady black and silver eyes, taking the slices slowly and eating each with the careful precision of a toddler choosing the best cupcake from the box. She was a sweet bird, really, but her beak seemed even sharper for Mrs Wilson's comments in the shop.

Mrs Wilson brought two cups over, setting them on the table. "She's already forgiven you, it seems."

"I think it's the chips."

"Probably." Mrs Wilson sat heavily in her tall-backed chair, the high wings flanking her head, and taking her tea up to her chest before she looked me over. "I am worried about you, Kathryn."

"Because of the fire?"

"And that, yes. Because I haven't seen you with people like this in all the time you've been here. You landed in Avon-on-Lee as an orphan and have done well for yourself. I'd hate to think that was because you were up to no good."

"I've not been running drugs, or anything like that. I wouldn't be as stressed about a new carpet if I had that kind of money."

"Hm." She sipped her tea, stony eyes watching me over the lip of the cup. She had lovely grey eyes, a deep hint of blue in there, but they were cross seas currently.

"I'm being serious. You know I came here after my mother passed, and that's true. I was alone enough."

"With a fiancé who didn't come to help you." She lowered her cup.

"I didn't want him to. I wanted to be on my own feet. His father came and offered, before I moved here, and I told him to go boil his head."

She laughed at that, and Coconut ruffled her feathers. I fed her another chip. "That sounds more like you. So, what has changed?"

"Bastian's father has passed, so he needs to take over the business. That means we need to be wed, in terms of the contract."

"Is his mother still alive?" I nodded. "She's not released you from it?"

"No. You would think she would, but it would be an offence to the dead. Both our fathers."

Mrs Wilson hummed, reaching out to stroke Coconut. The other birds were in their cages, in the shared room. I could hear the trill and flapping of them through the corridor. "You would think she'd see living people as more important than the dead."

"You would."

A knock disturbed us, making Coconut squawk, and I gave her another chip to examine as I went to the door. Seb was standing outside with my laptop. I opened the door, taking it from him, and he gave me a lopsided smile.

"You alright?" he asked.

"We're good. Coconut seems to be happy with the gift."

"Good. Let me know when you're ready to go. I'll keep tidying up downstairs."

"Will do. Thanks." I took the laptop from him, pecking a kiss to his cheek for show. He grinned, winking at me as he turned to walk down the steps.

I took the bag back into the living room, finding Coconut on the arm of Mrs Wilson's chair as I returned. She was preening Mrs Wilson's cardigan, a true sign she was content from my other visits up, and I smiled at them as I took my seat again.

"That your laptop?"

I nodded, perching on a seat to fish the machine out of the case. "Yes, so I can submit a claim. I'm going to have to have the shop boarded up for a week, probably, to get it dry enough to get a fresh carpet."

"Sounds about right. Will they come back and try again?"

Ouch. Before I answered, I chewed the inside of my lip. "I don't think so. I'm staying with him in the meantime, just in case, so that should take them away from here. Avon-on-Lee I mean."

"Is it to do with you marrying him? Does someone not like you?"

"It's to do with him. I'm ancillary, I think you could say." I tapped the laptop into life, navigating to my insurance provider.

"So you're going into the heart of the beast rather than running away like a sane person. That doesn't seem much like you, Kathryn."

I tried to cover my snorted laugh as a cough. "The enemy of my enemy is my friend. I've more chance of surviving with him than without, currently."

"That's hardly good to hear." She took to her cup again, watching me over the lip of it while she took sips of tea.

I started my claim while keeping half an eye on her, trying to find the nicest way to present it. "Better the town is safe than not, no? And Seb's a good man. Careful and cautious. Very determined to look after me."

"He laid hands on you?"

"No, not at all." I shook my head, looking up at her.

"Why do you have bruising on your neck then?"

I clenched my jaw. No real way to answer that which wouldn't worry her. "I was attacked at home. Someone waiting for me, when Seb took me back. He helped get me free."

She stared at me for a long minute; the silence only broken by Coconut ruffling her wing feathers. "That is not safe, Kathryn. How do you know that wasn't someone he'd sent to spook you into going back with him?"

"He wouldn't."

"He shows up on your door with a story about his dad dying and you don't think he would do something untoward? I've seen men like that in the hospital. I know they do wicked things even when they're crying that they'd never hurt their woman."

"Seb isn't like that. He doesn't do that sort of work. I know what you mean, and I can see why you'd think it, but he's not. I grew up with him, until we left, and I know he's not a wicked man."

"He didn't come see you in eleven years. Not even when your momma passed away?"

I shook my head. "It was complicated."

"I bet." She tutted, fussing over Coconut before she spoke again. "I don't want you mixed up in something dangerous. Arson and attacks, I tell you.

When you've had a successful business and a good life, here. Quiet. I knew there was something unusual about your past, but I didn't expect this."

"I didn't get a choice." I looked out the window, to the long street of shops. This time of morning it was bustling, a mill of people and vehicles. "I was promised as a child. There's a duty to uphold that, even if it's just for a while."

"Divorce?" I nodded. She tilted her head to one side, nodding a little. "If you're thinking that way, fine."

I glanced back at her. "Fine?"

"I know a thing or two about divorce. One of my ward sisters retrained to work in family law. She helps a lot of us about issues our children and grandchildren might have. She could see you right. And if she don't, I know my drugs still, I'll see you right."

I had brief visions of her serving a comatose Seb up to her birds and decided that was too much for today. "Okay, so you're less worried."

"I'm not happy, don't mistake that." She cooed at Coconut, scratching the little section of fuzzed skin above her beak. "But you're thinking practically. I like that. Will he expect you to give up the shop?"

"No. When I can reopen, I plan to. He knows that."

"You trust him?"

"Yes. If he wanted me barefoot and pregnant, I'd be gone."

"Good girl. Fine. But if you don't come back to see me in a week, I will call the police, so make sure you are coming back. I have photos of their cars and number plates."

I laughed at her, taking a sip of the tea she'd made us. It glowed warmly as I swallowed, the idea of her stalking their cars before she confronted them so funny to me. Of course, she was looking out at them. Sweet, terrifying woman.

"I will come back. Some of the family might help me with the shop, so you'll have time to meet them too, at least while we're repairing."

"Good. You've taken too much care with that little shop to see some idiot ruin it. Arsonist or fiancé."

"I think you'll like Seb once you get to meet him."

She shook her head at me. "I've met him. I didn't think much."

"Maybe a cup of coffee. Or dinner, sometime. You can come over to my house."

"Hm. Maybe."

I closed the laptop lid, form submitted, so I was simply awaiting an email or call back from them to see what they needed. "We can discuss it when I drop in again, yeah?"

"Yes. Are you going?"

"Yes, not much more to do except take photos and wait to hear from the insurers. We'll get the shop secured, then head back."

She stood up, letting Coconut hop onto one wingback of the chair. "I'll take in any packages, but don't be cluttering my house up. I expect them to be picked up at least weekly."

"No problem at all, Mrs Wilson. Thank you." I leaned into give her a hug.

"Just you be careful." She patted my back. "I've seen too many women run off with silly ideas of romance. I don't want you caught up in trouble."

"I will take care. Promise." We parted, and I grabbed my laptop bag up, shouldering it. "And I'll bring more chips for Coconut next time, too."

"Not every time. We don't want her getting spoiled." Mrs Wilson stroked Coconut's head, and the shine in those little eyes told me bringing banana would be a wise choice.

~

I found Seb on his own, taking photos of the damage to the shop. The second car was gone, so I presumed Fred and Daniel were off doing something else.

"You okay in there?" I called as I came in.

"I'm fine. Have you been released?"

"Yes. She wants to see me once a week, and she's not happy, but she's not going to report me as kidnapped."

"That's reassuring." He was bent low down, photographing the starting point of the fire. It gave a prime glimpse of the way his black jeans stretched over him and I turned away so I wasn't being indecent.

"She's taken photos of the cars, though. So she will call something in if she doesn't see me."

"It's nice to have such caring neighbours."

It was. As I looked around the shop, I chuckled and shook my head. I didn't need to go into the office for the security footage, that was backed up to a cloud account, but it held my folder of everything. I should take it to get more info for the insurers. That would mean seeing the poor dead thing again, and I sighed at the thought.

"How are you feeling?" Seb stood up, pocketing his phone as he came closer.

"Not like I'm going to be sick anymore. Fred was super sweet about that."

"He's a good guy, hands on. Him and Daniel are off to get wood to board the window up, and some dehumidifiers. They can stay here to clean up today."

"You don't need to do that. I don't want to be interfering with things."

Seb shrugged. "It's a safe job. I'd say have them keep the door open, but not with the carpet." He leant forward to squelch the water. "Maybe once things dry off. I'll pay for the refurbishment."

"You don't need to do that, I have insurance."

"I do. This wouldn't have happened if they didn't align you with me."

"The message does seem to show that, yes. And that they know what I go by, which is creepy. Poor baby, being killed for something so horrible."

"It's roadkill." I blinked at him, tilting my head to one side. "I smelled, to be sure. It's too rotten to be something just left overnight. And there are tread marks on the fur at the back leg. "

I winced at the thought of smelling that, given how bad it had been when I opened the door, but nodded as I looked back at the office. "Okay, so they got a dead cat to scare me. That's a little better, I guess?"

"Not really, but at least you know it wasn't harmed because of you. Seems like something you would be worried about."

"Yeah." Of course, I didn't want something killed because of me, cat or anything else. "I'll need to go in and get something from there."

"Want me to?" He touched my elbow, drawing my attention back to him. "If you don't want to see it again, I can go in."

"I mean, it won't bite me. Dead things aren't the problem. Someone alive is."

"I'll go in with you then. We can grab that and anything else you need, then go looking for your dress."

"What about the guys?" I asked.

"They can secure a shop on their own. Anyone tries anything I'm sure Mrs Wilson will have them bang to rights."

He wasn't wrong.

CHAPTER 17

Shopping took us back the way we had come, about forty minutes outside of Avon-on-Lee to a large commercial area I'd ventured up to a once or twice a year during my time here. It was expensive, somewhere with a mix of boutique shops and huge designer stores that had security flanking the front doors.

While I had done well with my business, it was not a place I came without a specific thing in mind - and a tight budget - which we did not appear to have this time around.

"Where do you want to look?" I asked as we parked up.

Seb shrugged. "Wherever you would like, there are a few places here. I know Marie had her eyes on one of the little places, Lily White, or something like that."

"Never heard of it."

"You haven't been looking for dresses on the off chance?" He winked as he said it, sliding our fingers together. It was easy, doing this part, like we were back to being kids playing at what we'd be now. The thought stung, but I pushed it away with a smile.

"Can't say it's been at the top of my list. It's usually new display cases or if I want to do work at the back of the shop to give me more room for stock. Half of it's in my house, as you saw."

"It's a good little shop. You use the space well."

"Thanks. I try."

"When we get the new carpet, maybe we should look at getting some standing displays, those big cube things you get? They'd let you keep the rotation going longer."

"I've thought about it, but it screws with the flow of the space. The open plan lets people wander more organically."

"Good point. Maybe some of those standing ones, then, so you can move it around without taking up the walkways."

"You getting eyes for my shop?" I choked back a laugh, the image of Seb throwing boxes of books around totally ridiculous in my mind's eye.

"No more than any businessman would. I can appreciate what you've been doing with it, and I'm thinking about what I would do. I'd want to have more stock too, like you say, and I'd want to differentiate the stationery. Get in some notebooks. The girls are always after them."

"Yeah, they're wonderful gifts. I have a few, but not many."

"You're careful with it, I like that." He led us inside, walking up to a map of the place. It was spread across two floors, with the boutiques mostly located upstairs. I ran my eyes over the list of names, spying the one he had mentioned and a few others; '*To Have and To Hold*', '*Best Dress*', '*Vows and Vixens*'. That one made my eyebrow rise, and I noted the location on the map. Not too far from the Lily one.

"Here's the one Marie mentioned." I poked the map.

"Do you want to go there first or check out some of the designer places?" Seb asked.

"Boutique would be good. I doubt the designer places will have my size off the rack."

"What do you mean?"

"Broad shoulders makes me a higher size. It's fine, I'm used to it, but it's not a good feeling to be told there's nothing in the shop that fits."

He hummed, glaring at the board. "No, that's horrible. I didn't realise shoulders did that so easily for women's stuff. I know about pockets, but I didn't think of that."

"Such are the perils of buying off the rail. It's fine, I don't mind. Plus, buying boutique means it's helping a small business, way better."

"Really?"

"Seriously. I'm always in favour of helping with a small business. Naturally."

"Naturally." Seb nodded absently, scratching his chin with one thumb before he shook himself a little.

"I'm sorry, Kat. Hardly the sort of experience you want for your wedding."

"Don't stress. Just take notes for the next one, so your proper lady has plenty of time."

"Don't say it like that. You're proper."

I batted his shoulder, resisting the urge to roll my eyes at him. "You know what I mean."

"Hm. Come on."

We took the escalator up, wandering along the upper floor as we checked the shops one by one. Lily Whites was at the far end of the walkway, with some of the others studded between perfume shops and jewellers with sparkling displays.

I hesitated at one window, eyes caught on an earring and necklace set. It was a simple style; a set of diamonds sat in a pear cut pendant, with a vibrant purple stone set at the pointed base, the same rich shade as a plum in autumn. They all had the same design - an almost art déco feel in the sharp edges - and they caught the light like a stream on a summer's day, twinkling away under the bright LEDs.

"Seem something you like?" Seb asked, joining me.

"Just something pretty. It'll be pretty expensive from here too, I bet," I said. They really were beautiful, much fancier than I had any need for, but the purple kept my gaze.

"Which is it, the pearls?" He pointed to a set of natural water pearls above where I was looking, a stormy grey string with flecks of green and purple within. They were beautiful as well, but they hadn't caught my magpie gaze like the set had.

"No, that diamond and purple set," I pointed, trying hard not to touch the glass. No one liked fingerprints on a splendid display. "They're lovely. Totally inappropriate, I have no reason to get them, but look at that shine. They're gorgeous."

"You want them?" Seb asked.

"I mean, they're very nice. Probably too much, though. Come on, we need to get a dress." He lingered at the window and I tugged him along by the fingers, drawing him away.

"I'd get you them, if you wanted them."

"I know you would. And I do, but I'll come back for them at some point. I come up here once or twice a year. I'll save up and get them next time."

"As you wish." He said, glancing back. "Where do you want to look first?"

"*Vows and Vixens* sounded quite funny. I presume they're going to be scandalous though, so we should check out Lily Whites."

"We can stop over at the first place if you like. I have no idea what options they'll have, either."

"You weren't looking at dresses on the off chance?"

He laughed, shaking his head at me before he brought my hand up to kiss my knuckles. "I deserved that one, huh?"

"Hundred per cent."

"You're goofy, you know. I forgot how much fun you were."

It caught me off guard, such a simple honesty, and I stuttered before I answered. "Never had a thought I didn't voice. Runs in the family."

Seb grinned, and it lit up his whole face like he was in sunshine. "I like it. You keep me on my toes."

"Someone has to. I saw the way you flung yourself at Josh. You run into everything like that?"

"Only where someone's being hurt." His eyes were honest too, almost prying with how gentle they were.

I looked away, sighing. "It was partly my fault. I broke his nose. Tends to piss a guy off."

"Doesn't excuse what he did. I expect Will to apologise for him at the ceremony."

"I'm sure they will. They want to keep on your good side, after all. Since you have numbers."

"They should behave. Might be some roughhousing when everyone's changed, but there's not been any attacks."

"Glad to hear it." My mind went briefly to Marie and her waiting news. I didn't know how that worked with the change, other than she would be carrying still. I quietly hoped for her, my hand flat on the softness of my tummy. She'd made it to four months. Daniel would keep her safe, surely.

We had arrived at the shop, a long and low windowed space that took up the end of the corridor we had walked along. The display showed a selection of mannequins styled in various dresses – glowing white meringue skirts, slinky mermaids, shining cream silk. Inside, I spotted a stylised tree, probably a sculpture, with long branches reaching across half the ceiling. White blossom hung and tumbled from them, giving some areas partial privacy, and the soft lighting made it all thrum with an ethereal, delicate radiance that had to make the mirrors more forgiving.

"I can see why Marie wanted to go here," I said.

"It looks… special. Nice." Seb nodded, face unreadable as he squinted through the window. "I don't see anyone else in. I have to nip and make a call. Can you talk to them and I'll be back once I've spoken to Daniel?"

"Sure. See you inside."

He took his phone out and stalked off, back the way we'd come. I laughed to myself as I went into the shop. The air was cool, probably for maintaining the dresses, and the walls were lined with large mirrors, their frames were all old wood and antique style gold, rich as warm as whiskey. At the far end, I could see a couple of doors covered with heavy curtains - I presumed they were the changing rooms.

A woman appeared at the far end, thin as a whippet and eyebrows popping up when she saw me. "I'm so sorry. Have you been waiting long?" Her hair was vibrant red, nothing close to natural, and cut in an angled bob that could have shredded paper, it was so sharp. She made a line for me, discarding the book she had been holding behind the corner.

"It's okay, I just got here."

"Good, I would feel terrible if you were having to wait on me. How can we help today?" She'd reached me now, little kitten heels quiet on the polished wood floor.

"I'm going to level with you – I'm getting married tomorrow. I had my dress picked out, but someone set fire to my shop last night and the dress was there, so my fiancé didn't see it. It's ruined and I need to find one today."

"Oh my goodness, girl, what a disaster!" The woman's face blanched, a hand covering her immaculate lipstick – a vibrant red to match her hair.

I slid my phone out, one thumb texting Seb my lie so he wouldn't mess the story up. "We're pretty stressed out. He's here with me, he's making calls to the folk helping us try to salvage things at the shop, so he will join us, but can you let me know what you have in my size?"

She quickly looked me over, giving a brief nod. "We'll have options for you, honey, no problem. Are you sure you want him to see, though? It's bad luck."

"We don't much believe in luck, given everything." I should feel guilty about lying here, but in terms of a cover story, it was almost true. We were stressed – or at least I was. There had been a fire at my shop. We were getting married tomorrow. I left out the part about wolves and murder and we'd all be the better off for it.

She nodded, eyebrows popping up in then dipping again. "No, well, I suppose that's fair. What's your man's name?"

"Seb. Bit taller than me, dark blond, dressed in dark colours." I held a hand up to show his height.

"Right, I'll keep an eye out for him, and we can look at options in the meantime. How about that? I'm Ricki, by the way." She held her hand out. Lovely nails, sharp as cat's claws and done it a neat reverse French manicure. Those had to cost.

I shook her hand. "Thanks Ricki, I'm Kat."

"Cute, Kat and Seb, I love it."

She led me deeper into the shop, past rows of dresses with their skirts fanning out like lines of ballerinas waiting to dance. The lighting was gentle, warm enough to make the gems and material glow but not show too many imperfections in the looming mirrors.

"They must keep you guys busy," I said.

"Not as much as we'd like, but we do okay." She winked, all easy smiles. "So, do you want a dress like your lost one or something different so it's not upsetting?"

I hummed, looking around at all the choices. My stomach twisted at the idea of trying them on, a pantomime dress-up of what should be important. "I think I'd like to go for something quite specific."

"Tell me all about it, and I will do what I can."

CHAPTER 18

This was how Seb found me with a selection of four dresses, evaluating them alongside Ricki's sharp eye. She had jettisoned my first instinct, a simple shift style white gown, and instead had brought a selection through into the faux-blossom solitude of the back of the shop. We had whittled those down to the current four, which now sat like sentinels as we discussed the options of each.

The first was as fragile as a frosted leaf fallen from a tree, all lace and delicate detail work, the gossamer material flowing in a full skirt and high neckline with an ornate, fastening collar. Sweeping sleeves trailed down to about the hips, thinning as they went like wisps of mist. It was dramatic, to my eye, but beautiful, and the skill in the work was clear.

The second was much more straightforward, a warm cream silk number that was almost the same shade as a crème brûlée with an A-line skirt that skimmed down into a short train. It had wide straps, almost like a tea dress, and it shone like a pearl under the welcoming glow of the lights.

The third, a wildcard, was a flapper style dress which looked like it would reach my mid-thigh, barely, and sagged with beads. It rustled as Ricki brought it in, the click of the detail work almost as loud as the art déco pattern which twirled around the bodice and demanded a level of attention I did not think I could stomach. She had paired it with a soft grey fur shrug, the lustre of it reminding me of the pearls Seb had mentioned earlier.

The last, and possibly most beautiful, was a mermaid tailed gown that had crystals studded around the skirt like a night sky. They twinkled with a cold light, creeping their way up the material to swirl into a fixation point at the princess neckline. That would need a shrug too, to cover my shoulder and chest, but it was almost ethereal in the way it glittered.

"Sorry to keep you," Seb called. He peered at the discarded rail of dresses, then back to me, smiling when he saw I was with company. "I'm Seb."

"So I hear. Ricki." She waved at him, immediately back to the selection. "I think you should try them on and see how they feel."

I raised my brows at her. "All four?"

"Yes, all four! This is your rescue dress. That means we need to be sure it's a good match. Your old one may have gone up in smoke, but we want this one to be a close second."

"I think she's right," Seb said. I scowled at him for the betrayal and was met with the smuggest grin back.

Ricki nodded. "You try them on and I'll see about some other accessories. Do you need shoes?"

"Yes," Seb said before I could answer.

"That would be lovely, thank you," I said.

"Alright, I will return. I trust I can trust you to help with zipping?" She fixed Seb with an assessing glare, and he nodded. "Good. Behave."

"Behave?" he repeated as she went off into a backroom.

"Apparently some couples get over amorous. Overcome with the beauty of the dress."

"Oh, right. I'll try my best to behave, then." He stepped into the privacy of the sheltered spot, standing beside me as he reviewed the dresses. "Do you have a favourite?"

"I'd just wear a white church dress," I said, with an exaggerated sigh, "But there are all very nice. I'm not sure which I would go for."

"Best do as the lady suggests then and see how they feel. I'll be on hand for zipping."

I blinked at him, then nodded. Not much point being bashful about it when he'd be seeing me in it tomorrow. "Sure. First, I have to send Marie pictures. She wants to know what I'm considering."

"Does she now?"

"Only seemed fair since you banned her from the shopping trip." I winked at him to lessen the tease, and he took it with half an eye-roll.

"You're as bad as her."

“What a shock,” I said. I took pictures of each dress and the detail work of the impressive parts, sending them in a little flurry of messages. She could respond when she had time. “Do you have a preference?”

He looked them over again, biting his lip as he did so. It looked so careless, utterly natural for him to be surrounded by white flowers and golden light, like he was doing this for real. Like it wasn’t a one day rush to cover ourselves, chased by a full moon and the memory of sharp knives. I shivered a little, rubbing my arms to dispel the goosebumps.

“It is cool. For the silk, yeah?”

“Yeah. How’d you know that?”

“One of mates for a while was a tailor, very particular about garment care. I was sad when he moved away. Come on, let’s try these and see what you like.”

“Alright. I’ll try the dangly one first.”

“Which?”

“With the arms.” I pointed to the first one, and he nodded, face carefully neutral, not an inch being given. I resisted the urge to roll my eyes. “You can say what you think, you know.”

“I don’t want to influence your choices.”

“Bold of you to assume you would manage that.”

He snorted a laugh, shaking his head at me. “Fair point, beautiful. It has never worked yet, has it?”

“Save the sweet words for the dresses. Do you hate any of them? Let’s try that instead.”

"I'm less keen on that one." He pointed to number three. "It's magnificent beadwork, but a bit too flashy. And if you need to run, the skirt will ride up."

"Need to run?"

He shrugged. "We have to be prepared for many things. An attack at the wedding is unlikely, but still."

"By that logic, surely it would be the best one then. Easier to run quick."

"I'll be sure you don't have to." He leant in and pressed a kiss to my hair, his chest pressing against my back. "That's one of my undertakings, as your mate. I'll always defend you."

The words rippled through me like a crashing tide, tugging my heart. He would defend me. Of course he would. That's who he was. Careful, protective, precious. It would be so easy to believe him, to give into the little game that we were doing this for real. And it was real, real as the material of the dresses in front of me, but not genuine. Not sincere. It felt too wrong, playacting this part, and I pushed the curls of comfort away as I stepped towards the dresses.

"Let's try this one first, then." I picked up number three. "That way, if it is as bad as we think, it can be discarded."

It was. The dress was beautiful, and the light rippled over the detail work like a sunshine in a field, but it sat perilously high on my long legs and if I turned too quickly, there would be a scandal. Not the choice for me then.

I glanced at Seb, who gave me an appreciative whistle but shook his head. "We could buy that too, for later on? Perfect honeymoon dress."

"Shut up. And unzip me." I turned away from him, watching him approach in the mirror. "So you were right. Any other's you're less fond?"

He wrinkled his nose in thought, reviewing the remaining contenders. "I don't like the one with drooped sleeves. Might go on fire."

I blinked at him in the mirror, his eyes on my back as he undid the zip. "Are you going to be shoving me into candles?"

"Not intentionally, but there are kids. They do silly things."

"You're such a worrier." I slid out of the dress, passing it to him, and plucked up dress number one. It was near see through, except the silk slip within, and would require more help that the flapper style. "You'll need to help me with this one."

"Let me know what to do."

I stepped into the dress, slipping it higher until the skirt sat at my hips. "Hold the material here." I tapped my side. His hands were there in the instant, a gentle press to keep the silk from slipping down. I threaded my arms into the delicate sleeves, shimmying it down so I didn't risk the threads, then gently tugged the shoulder caps up. "Okay, zip me."

He did as asked, stepping back when the material closed around me. I reached back to fasten the collar, little buttons fiddly at this angle, and he brushed my hands away. "Let me."

I stilled, then dropped my hands so he could fasten them. The cool air of the shop only heightened how warm he was next to me, broad chest to my back, and I swallowed as the collar tightened.

"Thank you," I said.

"Is it too tight?" he asked. I turned to look at him, the dress tugging against my legs a little as I moved around. "The collar, I mean."

"It's closer than I would like." I looked back at the mirror. It was a stunning dress, but it looked like frozen spiderwebs on me, too pale and too delicate to seem like real. Some fairy tale gift, which would disintegrate before the night was out. "It's not a good style on me, anyway."

"No?" He tilted his head, brows up.

"The neckline's too high on my throat, and the detail work is nice, but it looks fussy."

"As you say, beautiful. You'd outshine any of these dresses, anyway."

"Listen to this smoothie." Ricki reappeared, a blessed lifebelt in the storm of what we weren't saying. "No wonder she's still marrying you after a fire. I know brides that would have run a mile. They'd see it as a bad omen."

"We don't much believe in luck in my family," Seb said. To call his smile wolfish would be a step too far, and a disservice to the deliberate politeness he was presenting, but there was a flash of something sharp at his teeth.

"Not after all this, I bet," Ricki said. She led out a selection of items on one of the long tables nearby: shoes and jewellery, fascinators and what looked like a jacket, or maybe a blazer. It caught my eye enough that I moved closer, away from Seb, so I could inspect it.

"What's this?" The item wasn't the same delicate lace as the dresses: it was more of a tule that showed my fingers underneath it as I handled the piece. Pearls had been sown on in a scalloped pattern, like someone had been painting waves on a sea background, and they covered the whole material in the dipping, shining pattern.

"That is a topper – it's a very popular accessory for simpler gowns. You wear this over a plainer dress to give it a little pizzaz," Ricki said. "How are you having your hair, do you need new accessories for that?"

"Yes, we will, please." I was still looking the topper over, running my fingertips lightly over the bumps of the pearls. "My hair's going to be down now, so something to keep it neat would be great."

"I'll be back with tiaras; you keep on going." She winked at me as she vanished again, and Seb joined me at the table.

"You like that." It wasn't a question, as he nodded at the topper.

"I do. It's so… I don't know. I like how tactile it is."

"It would look lovely on you. The pearls, I mean."

"It's not great for the dresses, though."

"Maybe with that one." He pointed to dress two, the simpler silk number. The warm colour would make the pearls glow; he wasn't wrong there.

"Do you like that one?" I asked.

"It's my favourite of the bunch."

"Now you tell me!" I batted his shoulder, and he laughed, shaking his head.

"The diamonds on the other one are beautiful, but that skirt isn't safe. You can't run in it either."

I rounded on him, twisting on my foot so I could poke him in the chest. "Okay, next Mrs Weir, don't say things like that. I get it, I do, but my man. You cannot." I caught his chin in my hand, turning him to meet my gaze and shaking my head at him. "Tell her how beautiful she'll look gliding down the aisle, that she'll be breathtaking. Or that she looks like she could kill a man in it. Depends on your lady, I suppose. But don't do this bit."

He was so still under my hand I lessened my grip, lest I'd been too hard. "You're gonna kill me, Kat."

"What?" I took my hand back, ducking my head to break our eye contact. It was stupid to get so handsy, he wasn't doing anything except being careful.

"Saying things like that." He shook his head. "Try the dress on. I think you'll look breathtaking."

"Thanks." I bit the inside of my cheek to keep any further sarcasm in. "I'll need your help with the topper. It fastens at the back."

"I'll be right here for you."

My heart clenched, the gentleness of the comment as soft as the silk. "Thank you."

I slid into the dress, turning to let him zip me up, then threaded my arms into the topper. Shimmying it down to my chest, I let him button me up, four little links at the back that let the material sit softly against my skin.

Turning to the mirror, I inspected the result. The topped sat across the dress like sand across a dune, shifting and glittering but seeming utterly like it belonged, seamlessly inter-playing with the silk beneath. Even when the scalloped end seam hung at the line of my sternum, it seemed natural, like the pearls would flow out. No one would see patches of the dressing on my sternum, especially if I added some foundation over the edges.

"I told you it would look amazing," Seb said. I looked up at him in the mirror. He'd stepped back a touch, and crossed his arms as he looked me over.

"You'll be the most beautiful woman in the room. No one could hold a candle to you."

"You sound soft," I said, but there was no heat to it. It felt so intimate to have him there, watch the way his eyes took in the shape and flow of the dress. Like he was etching it into his mind. "It's an excellent combination, though. You were right." I splayed my hand on the silk, just underneath the pearls, to change the light.

"I think it's perfect."

"We should go for this, then." I turned to look at him as he stepped closer, causing a bump as we connected. He grabbed my waist to ensure I didn't go backwards, his hands bringing me flush. I blinked at him, suddenly so close I could count his eyelashes, and he stilled as he had before.

"I agree," he said, soft as a whisper. "We should go for it."

I opened my mouth to speak, but the words tripped up - lost somewhere between the way his eyes were as golden as sunset sunshine under these soft lights and the way his tongue slid out to wet his lower lip. It would be so easy. At least we looked like a genuine couple.

"I think you're right. You have a good eye."

"I think so." Seb ducked his head a little and for a tremulous moment our lips could have met, before he pulled back. "Everyone will love this."

I nodded, ignored the wavering in my chest at how he said 'everyone'. This was all for the pack, of course. Expectations. That brought a twist to my stomach, to Marie's news. "I have an indelicate question to ask about that."

"Go on?" He hadn't stepped back, and I turned around so he could undo the topper instead.

"Will there be expectations about children?"

He blinked at me in the mirror like I'd slapped him. "How do you mean?"

There was no wholly safe way to ask this out in public, but I couldn't keep the worry in, so I chose my words carefully. "Pregnancies can be hard. Especially for people like me. Will there be a timeline that people have in mind?"

"No. There will be a lot of joy when it happens, but no one will chase after you with a ball of wool to ask when they should start knitting. Why do you ask?"

"Blood and peaches," I said, then caught myself. "It sounds stupid, but my family has this knock for knowing when someone is expecting. We smell blood and peaches, or dream about it. It's a dead giveaway. So I'll know. And I wondered if you would too."

"That's a neat trick."

"Serves us well enough." I smiled at him in the mirror, hoping it seemed natural.

It wasn't as if I enjoyed lying to him. He was so stupidly earnest, so keen to get on with these things we had to do. How could I be angry at that? How could I *lie*? But it was a lie or risk harm. Tell him what I was, really, what I had become, what his mother had been too afraid to tell him but pushed me to instead. As if I'd chosen it. At least we were all suffering together. There was some cold comfort in that.

I dropped his gaze in the mirror, tapping my shoulder. "Come on, help me out of this and we can get it before Ricki sells us the entire store."

"She's very good at it." He set his hand on mine, startling me into looking over at him. "Are you okay?"

I smiled again, huffing a laugh. "Fine, just ready to stop playing dress up. There'll be plenty of time for more tomorrow at the ceremony."

"I can't wait for people to see you in it. You'll look amazing."

"Thanks, Seb."

CHAPTER 19

The drive back should have been easy, our bounty loaded into Seb's car and ready to be unpacked once we reached the house. The front was full of the buzz of silence, our almost kiss loud against my skin, and doubt had set in like rot throughout my musings. I kept turning things over in my mind - laying my options open and closed like a book that couldn't hold my attention.

"You okay there, Kat?" Seb asked.

"Hm? Just thinking about ordering a new carpet." I brought my gaze back round into the car, smiling at him.

"Is that so?"

I nodded, trying to settle into a reasonable conversation topic. "It's not the end of the world. I have money. It's an unexpected thing."

"Are you feeling unsafe? Or worried about something?"

The question caught me off guard, snagging somewhere in my brain. "How does that connect to carpet?"

"We already spoke about the carpet, beautiful." He winked, shaking his head at me.

Heat flooded up my cheeks, but so did a smile. "Caught me. Sorry."

"What's on your mind?"

"I mean, a knife in a cat is pretty pointed. I feel better it was dead already, but there's still a distinct threat. And while I don't doubt your promise to defend me, I am wondering who wants that to be necessary."

"No secret enemies waiting in the wings?"

I huffed a sigh, my chest twisting. There was no one waiting in my wings. No family background, no cousins looking to pick through an inheritance, nothing.

"I mean, not that I know of. I'm sure I've pissed some people off by not stocking certain books on release week, but that's not enough to cause this. Which means it's probably tied in with you and what happened to your dad."

"Like Fred said, it would be green to assume this wasn't about us."

"And, honestly, that's a bit tricky to navigate."

"Trickier than when you were attacked at home?" Seb looked over at me, brows pinched.

I laughed, no actual warmth to it. "No, I suppose not. We've already had that conversation, too."

"What is it, then?"

"I don't feel good trading on other people's mercy. The idea that you'll have to be there to save me, or playing along with Marie that this is some big adventure when it's to keep us all safe until I can leave again." Marie had liked the dress. That was a small win, at least. She'd like the topper too, I could tell, something to sparkle a little.

"You don't have to. Leave, I mean." He pulled the car over to the side of the road, clipping the emergency lights. I missed the quiet of before, the press of this tension was like a needle behind my eye. We sat in silence for a beat, his gaze on the road while I kept mine on the dash.

I cracked first. "You can't say things like that, Seb."

"Why not?" He twisted on the seat, so his shoulder pressed into the back and he could see me properly.

"It's not fair."

"To who?"

"Either of us." I looked over at him, flinching away from the heat in his eyes.

"Why is it so bad?"

"We were kids! We were kids and then my dad was dead, and I we don't even know each other anymore." I hated the way it caught in my throat, the heat rushing up to spring at my eyes, and I covered my face with my hands so he didn't see how easily I was falling into tears. I couldn't do this, I couldn't do this to *him*. It wasn't right. But I also couldn't just roll over to get got because someone had issues with his father.

"Kat, beautiful, don't cry." Seb was so fucking earnest, so soft when he tried to pull me to him in the cramped space, and I shoved him away, pressing myself back against the door. He looked at me like I'd hit him, his mouth opening a little as if he would speak.

I shook my head at him. "Don't. I can't."

"Can't what?"

"I can't do this, Seb, I can't be what the pack needs me to be, and you're you, you're so you, and it breaks my heart."

"What does that mean?"

"It means it would be easy! This, us. You would be so easy to love, with your stupid fucking heart and your pretty smile, and you deserve better than this. You deserve someone to really love you, not just because it's easy."

I scrabbled for the door handle, launching myself out as if I could run away from the words I'd said. It was ridiculous and petulant, but I couldn't shake the look on his face when I'd pushed him away. The hurt that hadn't been there last night.

"Kat, wait!"

"I need a minute!" I shouted over my shoulder, long strides taking me away from the car and towards the tall, dark trees. The air was warm, even away from the tarmac, but the forest smelled alive, the green tang of sap and mulch overwhelming as I walked to the edge, leaned into a tree. I covered my mouth with my hand, struggling to keep my cries in, keep the burst of pain and adrenaline back. It wasn't fair, I shouldn't have said that to him. I shouldn't have been so stupid to have said that.

"Babygirl, you don't have to do this all alone." I jumped at the touch of his hand on my shoulder, too startled to protest when he turned me, pulling me into a hug. "Please, let me help."

I was too close to him to answer, my head pressed into his chest, his arms pulling me close. And try as I might, I couldn't stop crying. He shushed me, stroking my back with one broad palm and letting me soak his shirt. Shame twisted in with everything else, as hot as the tears scalding my face.

We stood like that until the tears stopped, and until my shivering sobs turned into a hiccup, then silence. Cars drove past but none stopped, the scene probably typical enough to warrant a lack of concern.

"I'm sorry," I said, eventually.

"You don't need to be sorry."

"I called you stupid."

Seb snorted a short laugh. "I think you said I had a stupid fucking heart, technically. I didn't even know hearts could do tests. Mine's probably dumb as a brick."

"You graduated, that probably translates."

"And you said my smile was pretty."

I rested my head against his chest, in the damp patch left by my tears. "I take it back. I'm not sorry."

"Good. You don't have to apologise for having feelings. Or nerves. What bride doesn't get nerves?"

I frowned up at him. "Even fake ones?"

"You're not a fake bride. You're a real person with real feelings and real fears. I know this must be scary. You've been away and you've had your own life. You deserve better than this as a wedding. But I will make it the best I can for you, if you let me."

"I can't exactly stop you. We're stuck in this together."

"Together is the best part. We're a team. The entire pack is, of course, but you and I are a team. Even if it's only for a while, until we sort things out. I'd like it to be longer."

I frowned at him. "Why?"

"I guess I just like you."

"Sounds suspect."

He raised his brows at me, shaking his head. "You're very good at making it seem easy. I wouldn't even know it was fake if you didn't keep telling me."

I laughed, holding back the roll of my eyes. "As if. You don't need to butter me up."

"I'm serious, you have everyone else fooled. I saw the way Josh looked at you, after he knew who you were. That was fear."

"I think that was the fight and him being afraid you'd kick the hell out of him. I don't think he was terrified of the big bad witch."

"Hrm, we'll see at the wedding." He stepped back, his hands on my shoulders. "Let's head back. You can show off the dress to Marie and we'll get through it. Maybe even have a good time. It's a wedding. They're meant to be fun."

"Sure. Sounds like a plan."

"I have something for you, by the way." He went onto his toes as he reached into both pockets, revealing a black box in each hand.

"What on earth?"

"Open them. This one first." He handed me the larger one, still small enough to sit in my palm. It was black velvet, with fine silver lines like vines making a border around the inside of the lid, and it was heavy enough to make me want to rattle it.

I ignored the impulse, instead opening the lid. Within sat the necklace I had been admiring in the shop window, twinkling even in the dappled light of the woods. "Seb."

"Kat."

"I thought you were calling Daniel."

"I did. Then I went and got these. They'll look amazing with the dress, if you want to wear them then, or just amazing on you. They shine like you do."

"I only shine because I'm pale."

"Hush, you goofball, and open the other one." Seb thrust the smaller box forward, and I found the earrings in there as well, winking back at me like pearls in an oyster. "I knew they'd look good on you, so I wanted you to have them."

I grinned as I shook my head, tracing the lines of the pieces. "You're daft, you know. I would have got them."

"I know you would, but I wanted to. So, I did."

It shouldn't have made my chest warm to hear him say that. It shouldn't have made me smile like a silly teenager, buoyed by a gift. But it did, and I did smile, pecking a kiss to his cheek. "Thank you. I'll wear them tomorrow, then. They'll go way better than some of my own."

"They are yours now, but yes. I'd enjoy it if you did that."

We walked back to the car together, close but not touching, and I tucked the boxes away in my bag. "Why are they in two boxes? Have I spoiled a surprise you were going for?"

He chuckled, ducking his head into a little shake. "No, I asked them to do that so I could hide them easier. Would look a bit obvious wandering back in with a proper gift box."

I laughed at his logic, nodding. "Even I might have noticed that, yeah. What's the plan for when we get back?"

"We should probably eat something, since it's well past lunch, then Marie and my mother will want you for the rest of the afternoon."

Of course, ceremony planning. Urgh. At least Gillian might pull me out of my misery. She hadn't been that bad this morning once my hurt had subsided. "As long as I can grab some time to deal with the insurance folk, no problem."

We got into the car, setting off again.

"Of course. And tonight, we will get left alone, so we can do whatever you want," he said.

"Oh?"

"It's considered a dry run for the honeymoon. We spend an evening getting to know each other, but we already know each other, so really it's a break in the planning for everyone to have a breather."

I cocked my head at him. "You won't be needed at work?"

"Victor has me covered all this week. He's been an enormous help getting everything set up."

"I imagine it's a mixed blessing for him."

"How so?"

"Well, it's good for the pack, as you say. And he's obviously going to be delighted for you, you're his best friend's son. But he's lost Michael, and John too, that must hurt. To see preparations you expected for your own kin and they're not there."

Seb hummed, biting his lip. "Are you thinking about your mother?"

"I hadn't been, at least consciously, but probably, somewhere, yes. It's not a shock she's not here, but it is a shame."

"Maybe you can talk to Victor about it. I know he's not the cuddliest of us but he saw you grow up as well. He knows the feeling."

"I suppose." It would be sensible to speak to him. Maybe even kind, something I hadn't been to him when my mother died. The thought sat ill about my shoulders, but perhaps that was the old grasp of grief settling in again. I would see what I could do.

CHAPTER 20

Back at the house, the afternoon blurred into evening as I was presented with food choices, music, decorations, and lighting. Marie and Gillian had made some decisions already, but for a wedding two weeks in the planning, they put it together well.

"We thought it would be good if you had input, but no one wants to plan a wedding at the drop of a hat," Marie said. She'd pulled out a huge ring binder, filled to the brim with cut outs and options, and flooded her coffee table with comparisons for us to pick from.

The wedding would take place in a marquee at the changing point in the woods. This would make the wild running later easier, and it meant we limited the decorating to the trees and the tent itself rather than having to bedeck tables and plan seating arrangements. It also meant while the rival wolves were going to be in the woods, they would not be in the houses of the pack, and I would be lying if I said that wasn't a relief.

Once we settled on what we liked, I left, going back over to find Seb in the kitchen. He was elbow deep in making a sauce, if the frantic stirring was anything to go by, shirt discarded to reveal the vest he wore underneath, and he was frowning at a well-worn copy of a cooking book I might have sold in Page Turner.

"You alright there?" I asked as I shed my coat.

"Not quite."

"You're looking at that book like you're going to start tearing chunks out of it."

"I'm making dinner, but the instructions for the sauce don't quite seem to work for me."

I joined him at the stove, peering over his shoulder to look at the page. It was a fish pie, according to the header on the page, and I could see there was a pan of mashed potato ready to go on the back of the stove. The evidence of sauce-based struggles was also strung about the kitchen counter – spilled flour, massacred tubs of butter, a green and white blur on the chopping board.

"You're making a white sauce?" I asked.

"Attempting to."

"Want me to help?" I asked.

He blew air up his face, shifting the pan from the heat so he could wipe his face. "This was meant to be a surprise."

"I'm surprised."

"A proper one." He shook his head at me. "Your mother used to make good fish pie. She's the only person I know who did. We're not exactly massive fish eaters in the pack. I thought it might be a nice way to have her close."

Sweet, sweet man. I rested my chin on his shoulder, shaking my head. "Well, lucky for you, she taught me how to make it. Cause you're making that all wrong." I pointed to the white paste in his pan.

"Oh?"

"You're adding the milk first; that's never gonna work. Needs to be butter, the flour, then milk. Like you're making a roux."

"Clearly, I am outclassed in the sauce department. I would be very grateful if you could show me."

He stepped sideways from the stove and I took his place, scraping the goo out and starting afresh after rinsing the pan. Taking the butter, I melted it over a low heat, letting it liquify before I added the flour and whisked it into browning, then sprinkled in what I could salvage from the chopping board. He joined me to watch the roux darken - standing behind me so he could see what I did - and then once it had achieved a golden brown, I added the milk a little at a time while whisking.

"The trick is to keep the movement going," I said, grabbing Seb's hand and placing it on mine over the handle. "You can do it with a spoon once you're used to doing it, but even with a whisk, it's an easy, repetitive movement."

"You make it a lot?" His breath was warm against my skin as he leaned closer, looking into the pan.

"White sauce? It's a great one to make. Sometimes I'd make it and have it on toast. Or to use as a dip."

"A dip?" He turned his head, chin running against mine.

"Sure. Like carrot sticks. It's not as healthy as guacamole, sure, but it's good. Where's the fish?"

"In the oven." He stepped away, opening the oven door and bringing a baking sheet of fish pieces over. I'd not even noticed a smell from them cooking when I came in. He must have had the windows open all afternoon to keep that hidden.

I smiled at him, nodding to the pot. "Add it in, and I'll mix it for you."

"This somewhat ruins the element of me making it for you, you know?"

"We're making it together. That's nicer, no?"

"Not quite what I had imagined, but yes. Sure." He shook his head at me, tipping the fish in. "Did you get everything sorted for tomorrow?"

"I think so. Marie already had most things covered; it was just giving my preferences. She's so organised, she'd make a great wedding planner."

"Don't tell her that. She might get ideas."

I laughed, coating the fish in the white sauce as Seb set the oven dish on the counter. "I'm serious. If she made it as easy as she's made this one, everyone would pay her. It's been the easiest shotgun wedding I've ever been part of."

"Got a few in the back pocket?"

I snorted, pouring the mixture into the dish for him. "Yeah, loads. Five before breakfast."

"Hm, should have checked that before Marie got busy, I suppose. Reckon we'll hold up?"

I pretended to think about it as we sprinkled vegetables over the mix, and Seb began to layer the mashed potato on top. "I reckon so. None of the others had werewolves."

"Ah, we have a unique selling point, excellent. Cheese?"

"Yes, please."

He sprinkled a liberal amount of cheddar over the top before scooping the dish away and popping it in the oven. He dusted his hands off, streaking white marks across his trousers and, I grabbed a towel, wiping the flour that had skimmed across his cheek and hair.

"Thank you," he said.

"You're welcome. Next time you decide to wage a war against the supply cupboard, let me know and I will assist before you're too deep in the trenches."

"How about a war report over a glass of wine before we eat, then?" He turned to the fridge, pulling out a bottle of white.

"That sounds like an excellent idea. You get this in special?"

He nodded, taking the cap off. "I thought, since we already know each other, it might be nice to have a catch up. Eat a familiar meal, have some wine, get a sense of what we want to happen tomorrow."

"Other than getting married?" I found two glasses and set them out for him to pour into. He filled them generously, though not overly so, enough left in the bottle for more with the meal.

"That is one of the few certainties. There may be others. An attack. A social challenge."

"Someone objecting because they're secretly in love with you?" I took the offered glass of wine.

"Not as likely, but if you think any swooning heartthrobs are likely to make a claim for your hand, please let me know. I hadn't planned for hand-to-hand combat but if needed…."

"Oh, will I have to fight anyone who seeks to claim you, too?"

"Do you want to?" He smirked, clicking our glasses together. "To fish pie."

"To fish pie." I sipped before I answered, letting the wine roll across my tongue. It was nicely chilled, dry without being acidic. "I could fight someone, but not sure I stand a chance against any of the wolf girls. Maybe if one of them went for my hair, but an actual fistfight, I bet they'd beat me into the grass."

"You wouldn't just break their nose?"

"Seems a bit rude."

"In a fistfight?" He laughed into his glass, shaking his head at me.

"Yeah, there are rules for ladies. No hair pulling, no earring pulling, no going for the eyes. All you guys do is no hits to the crotch. We have layers to worry about."

"Oh, I didn't realise there was such nuance. You have a lot of experience with these, too?"

I leaned back against the counter, holding the glass up as I watched the fluid catch the light. "I'll have you know book conventions can be very violent places. If you don't know the rules, you're dead on the convention hall floor."

Seb nodded, smirking as he leaned forward on the island. "Terrifying. Here was me thinking I might drag you into a world of danger and I'm ignoring that you're already a hardened warrior."

"It's okay, you've not lived the book shop life. How could you know?" We shared a beat of silence, easy against the whir of the oven and the bustle of people heading home outside. "Do you really think there will be an attack?"

"There shouldn't be. But, equally, someone shouldn't have killed my father, and yet here we are. I'd prefer to be prepared."

"You're very good about that. Being prepared, I mean." I took another sip of wine, nodding to the sink. "Your first aid kits are great. And you know what everyone can do. You were a natural with the pack this morning."

"You think so?"

"Yeah. Everyone's been so enthusiastic about you when I've spoken to them, or caught up with them. There's a good amount of new folk, but some of them know me. It's nice, in a way."

"In a way?"

"Lying doesn't taste good to anyone. I'm being careful to be gentle about what I share, but there's a lot to be said in the silences."

"You only have to say what you want to. No one will pry about your mother. If anything, I think they might feel bad that she's not here, but it's the same with me and my father. They'll mean to be respectful."

"I get it." I took another drink. "It comes from a good place. And we'll be as good as we can tomorrow and then people will talk about something else. Until they ask about my…. duties, would you say? The things my father did for the pack."

"We don't have to worry about them as much. When you left, we did other things. We can continue to do so."

"Will that be approved of, with me being here now?"

"Some people might grumble, but I've already said you have your business. As long as you're here for the things that matter, they'll be fine."

"The things that matter like full moons?"

"That. And holidays, celebrations. There's a lot of joy in the pack. If you're part of that, then they'll be there for you too."

My chest thrummed at the idea, a warmth entirely unrelated to the wine spreading under my skin. "We'll have to see if I'm here long enough for that. The pie smells done."

He nodded, setting his glass down. "I'll serve up if you set the table?"

"Sounds good." I put my glass down too, reaching into a cupboard to grab the plates for him. "Race you there."

CHAPTER 21

The pie was, without a doubt, excellent. Seb had got fantastic fish, flaky and delicate as I loaded it onto my fork, and the cheddar smelled like it would spark off your tongue.

"You really went all out," I said.

He shrugged, pouring more wine before he answered. "I wanted to show you what I could do."

I giggled at the frisson of joy that brought me and made a point of taking a bite before I drank any more. It would not do to be hungover at my own wedding. "Showing off that you're husband material?"

"Something like that." He smiled, sitting down to join me at the table. Sat across from each other like this it was intimate - a perfect date - but it was also familiar, easy like it had been when we stopped for burgers.

"As if you need to do that for me, you dafty. I'd have accepted take out."

"I know, but you don't have to. I wasn't raised to expect a wife who would wait on me hand and foot."

I nodded, pointing my fork at him before I ate more. "Now that doesn't surprise me. Much as your parents loved each other, I can't see Gillian letting you get away with little king syndrome."

He snorted, shaking his head at me. "That a technical term?"

"Hundred per cent. I always got told it was a good thing I wasn't born a boy. I'd have been brought up the same and have had a terrible time."

He tilted his head, setting his fork down while he took another sip of wine. "I, too, am glad you weren't born a boy. You're much prettier as a woman."

"Flirt." I ate more pie.

"I'm glad you've noticed."

"How could I not? A homemade meal, wonderful wine, that smile." I stretched my legs, brushing against his under the table. I quickly pulled mine back, shaking my head at myself. "Sorry."

"Don't apologise, it's fine. I enjoy seeing you a bit more relaxed."

"I could say the same about you, now you're not glaring at the book."

"Hm."

"It was a stupid way to do the sauce," I said with a wink. "I'd support you biting it. Maybe I'll even write mine down so you can use that in the future."

"I would like that. You could teach me, too."

"I damn near did, back there. You were close and watching."

"Maybe I was distracted." Seb's eyes flashed, just a little, and my breath came short in my throat. I could almost feel the heat of him again, how close he'd been in the shop, then again at the stove. I took a sip of wine to hide my reaction.

"Somehow, Seb Weir, I think it would take more than a repetitive wrist action to distract you."

He choked on his mouthful of food, grabbing a napkin to wipe his mouth. "Oh, full name getting pulled out. Was it that bad of a line?"

"Yes." I shook my head as I took another forkful. "I don't know where you learned to be so smooth, but it's quite impressive."

"Good to hear."

"Have you thought about what you'll do differently next time?"

He hummed, batting his lashes at me. "I don't plan for there to be a next time, if I can help it."

"You know, a woman could mistake that for a declaration of intent."

"Could you now?"

"I could." Seb smiled, giving a little shrug. He was infuriating, and here I was lapping it up. "And if I did, what would that mean?"

He took a sip of wine and I bit my lip at the way the candlelight played in his hair, the stretch of his neck as he tipped his head back. "What would you want it to mean?"

"That's not fair, I asked first." It was such a silly thing to throw back at him. I'd been throwing things at him all day, one way or another, and he kept batting them back.

"Just for a little while, why don't we try it?" he asked. He reached out across the table, tangling our fingers together.

"We're already eating your cooking."

"No, Kat. Why don't we try us? A real honeymoon period. You're going to be staying with us until things are resolved, and we're going to be married. Why don't we let it be a trial run?"

I set down the glass that had been part way to my lips, spinning the stem in my fingers. "Is that a good idea?"

"Why not?"

"It might make it hurt at the parting."

"Nothing says there has to be one."

"Seb."

He moved his hand higher, covering my hand with his. "I'm serious. Give us a shot. Give me a shot. You said yourself it would be easy."

"It would." My voice was so small, stuck behind my teeth.

"So do easy. Let's be together, and see what it's like."

"Why?"

"We've been promised for eleven years. Why don't we test it out? Neither of us has settled with someone else. You know the pack, and they know you. I know you." He squeezed my hand. "And you're still gorgeous."

"Hush." I looked away, heat flooding my face. Seb stood up, walking around to take my hands and kneel beside my chair.

"Kat, I'm serious. I believe we can do it. Why not give us a shot?"

A thousand responses died on my tongue. Because this was a lie. *I* was a lie. And despite that, something in my chest fluttered at the idea that I could do what he said; slot in with the life I left behind here and be part of what had been. Meeting his gaze, my chest wavered at how close he was, how easy it would be to lean in and finish what he had started this afternoon.

"What if it's not that simple?" I asked.

"Why does it have to be complicated?"

I closed my eyes, taking a deep breath. "Sometimes it is, even when we don't want it to be."

"Then, screw it." He cupped my cheek, and as I opened my eyes, he was leaning his forehead into mine. "I don't care, Kat. I know there are some things we might not share straight away. That's fine, we've had lives. Are you married to someone else?"

"No!" A startled laugh escaped my lips, and Seb grinned at me.

"Then it doesn't matter. Give me a chance to make this good for you, to show you what we can be. Please?"

I took a wavering breath in, staring at him. It would be a selfish, rotten thing to say yes, I knew that. I did. But he was here, and he was him, and it was so good to feel his hand on my cheek, the warmth of his gaze as it appealed to me.

"If I say yes--" I began. He surged forward, his lips tumbling onto mine and I couldn't stop the gasp as I pressed into him, hand going to his hair to hold him, feel him closer. I lost the time between my breaths as we stayed like that, the hand on my cheek pulling me gently forward, my fingers tangling in his hair as the kiss lingered.

We parted, cheeks flushed and lips tingling from the heat of us. Seb brought our foreheads together again, smiling as he pecked little kisses to my lower lip. "I've wanted to do that since this afternoon. I couldn't get it out of my mind. You were saying?"

I grinned at him, laughing a little. "I was saying, if I said yes, it would have to be on the understanding that it wasn't guaranteed. It's like a test run."

"I can be good with a test run." He pecked another kiss to my lips before he stood up and stepped away, back to his seat. "You don't have to tell me everything, beautiful. I don't expect you to. But I'm glad we can try."

"Me too." I picked my glass up, running a fingertip along my lower lip before I took a sip. "I didn't know you got so bold."

"I find I can be a lot of things for you, beautiful."

I shook my head, pushing my food around my plate a little before I dared take another bite. "It raises another question."

"Go on."

I tried to choose my words carefully, though I was already so flustered it simply came out as I thought it. "What do you want to do with the rest of the night?"

Seb hummed, sucking on his lower lip before he answered. "While I would love to continue where we left off, I think finishing that bottle and talking would be best. We still have the den Daniel made, ridiculous as it is."

"That would be nice. It was very sweet of him."

"Marie's trained him well. Runs rings around him, at times, but they're lovely."

"You sound fond."

He nodded, continuing to eat. "It's natural to want her to have someone good. Dad approved; though he always gave Daniel a hard time. Just to be sure. I feel great about their wedding, from what you've said."

"She'll be amazing, seriously. She's been so good with me." I bit my tongue so I didn't say anything more, taking a quick sip of wine.

"I'm sure it'll be impressive. She won't have done all of this and not have one eye on her own as well. Daniel will know that. And it's been nice for everyone, so having another one to plan for will be good too."

"You're quite the mother duck, you know?" I giggled, pouring more wine for both of us. "It's cute."

"Cute?"

"As a duckling." I winked, finishing the fish pie. "How about I wash up and you get the den ready, then? We can get cosy under the blanket and you can tell me what battle formations you have in mind for the flower girls."

Seb's head perked up, brows higher than he'd had them when we kissed. "Are we having flower girls?"

"I adore the fact you actually asked that question. No, no, we are not, but good to know you'd have a plan to arm the entire procession."

His shoulders slumped, and I couldn't tell if it was relaxation or embarrassment. "I was more thinking about how we would cover them if there was an attack."

"Of course, right, my mistake." I laughed, taking his empty plate away as I went towards the kitchen. I stopped at the door, looking over at him. "You know, if they attack the wedding, you're forgetting one thing."

"What's that then, beautiful?"

"Well, we'll have to sit them on my side, right? If they misbehave, I can go total Bridezilla on them."

He blinked a couple of times. "I can't tell if you're joking."

"Good." I winked, retreating into the kitchen before he could ask further.

CHAPTER 22

The day broke with sunshine and no headache, which was a good sign that I had eaten enough dessert to counteract the wine we had finished in the den.

I smiled at the memory: the warmth of Seb's arm pressed against mine as we laid on the adapted sofas, the way the fairy lights had shone across his skin. It was a silly indulgence to spend the night in, but it had felt good to relax with him, enjoy his company.

Sitting up, I rubbed the sleep from my face, sliding into the shower and washing up quickly. The wound at my shoulder blade hurt, but it wasn't as bad as I'd expected, and the cuts at my front could stand the water without the same wincing pain as yesterday.

Towelling off, I saw it was nearly eight, late enough that others would be awake, and I pondered my morning. I was going to be over at Marie's house all afternoon with preparations: much as Seb had seen the dress, I didn't want him to see the full look until the ceremony, so I was getting ready over there. And I was wearing trainers until we got to the clearing because screw doing that hike in heels.

That still gave me a few hours to kill, and while I could chase up the insurers, one of Seb's comments was lingering in my mind. Peering out the window, I searched for Victor's house, checking for signs of life.

Someone was moving around behind the curtains in the kitchen. I could see the familiar morning dance of breakfast and coffee being made. It would be rude to interrupt their meal, but maybe I could grab him for five minutes. Just to say my piece. He'd probably be expecting it anyway, as the officiator.

Probably.

I got dressed and went before I could double guess myself, marching over to the house in a neat top and skirt. I could look respectful.

I knocked on the door with a quick rat-a-tat, hoping not to waken anyone who wasn't already up, and waited. Rose answered – shorter, her strawberry blonde hair streaked with grey that wasn't there before, but she smiled like she always had.

"Kathryn, what a pleasure. What can I do for you?"

"I was hoping to have a quick word with Victor, if he's available? I appreciate it's early."

"Come in, I'll get him for you." She ushered me into the house, setting me in the kitchen, where the scent of coffee welcomed me like a cat around my ankles. I sat at the table, playing with my hands while I waited for company.

It was an immaculate kitchen - Rose was clearly diligent. The counters looked regimented as soldiers, and they bedecked the wall beside the window in family photos. I wandered over to look at them, unable to stomach sitting with my back to the door. I could say it was a side effect of someone having attacked me. Twice.

Rose had less grey hair in most of the images, smiling at the camera with an arm around Annabelle and Michael, her face alight with love. It was like a thunderclap, seeing Michael, but the wall was full of such affection, it was hard not to feel it pouring off. He had looked so young, despite being my age, and the captured joy was clear as sunlight.

"He was a handsome lad." Victor's voice caught me off guard, making me spin around.

"It's lovely to see him," I said.

"Rose said you wished to speak to me."

"Yes, sorry to come over so early. Can I take five minutes?"

"You can take ten if you wish. Come into the study." He opened the kitchen door and led me through to an ordered front room, desk and cabinets shiny from polishing. "What can I do for you?"

"It was two things, really. I wanted to speak to you about today, and, um…" I trailed off, trying to find the words. "And my family, I suppose."

"Your family?" He sat in the overstuffed chair beside the desk, motioning for me to sit on a large sofa that was tucked beside the window.

"I'm not sure how best to say it. You and Gillian are the closest I have to family, technically, though Mrs Wilson above my shop would probably stake a claim, too." I laughed, anxiety tripping over my tongue. "I don't have anyone else here for me. No one to walk me down the aisle, or those things. And I'm not asking you to do it. I know you're representing John in your role, but it's just… Lonely, I suppose." There was a heat in my eyes, a betraying heat that I knew meant I was close to tears. It was so stupid to get upset at the old pain, but here I was.

Victor hummed. "And you thought I would know the feeling, having lost Michael."

"Yes. Is that wrong of me?"

"No, of course not. If we can share joy, we can share grief as well. Such is the way of a pack."

I huffed air, nodding as I wiped my eyes with the back of my hand. "I suppose so."

"It is not too late, if you wish to change that."

"What?"

"You aren't married yet. If you are truly afraid of us, and this," he twirled his hand to show the office, "You can still step away. I know Bastian is doing this for the good of the pack, but that is his obligation rather than your own."

I had not expected Victor to be a voice of reason. The shock of it settled across my shoulders, my words slow to come. "It would feel wrong to run away."

"Like your mother did?"

The comment stung like a slap. I bit my lip before I spoke, swallowing. "She thought it was best, given my father's death. If that was right or wrong, I can't say. She didn't tell me the rest until she died."

He tilted his head at me. "The rest?"

"Me. The rest about me. I think she wanted me to be grown before I knew about it."

"Any parent would try to protect their child."

"You were a parent then, too." It was a cruel thing to say, an unnecessary harshness when his son's death was still recent, but that little rage in my heart that I had locked away was back and burning behind my ribs.

Victor nodded. "I was. I didn't have Annabelle then, though. Now I suspect I may have chosen differently if I did. Annabelle has made me rethink a lot of things."

I let my head fall forward, my braid slipping around one shoulder to hang down beside my neck. It should have been a good thing to hear, but it left bitterness seeping across my tongue.

"Why did you do it? All of you, my father, too. Why did you think it was okay?"

"We didn't do it lightly, Kathryn. Not at all. We felt it was necessary for the pack. And it pained your father to keep it from your mother. For a while I wondered if it was her that killed him, out of fury for what he did to you, but she wouldn't have run if she had. Sophie had more to her than that."

"She would never." My teeth sank into my cheek, pain to focus me on keeping in the venom I wanted to spit at him.

"I don't believe never, she would have killed to defend you. But I don't think she did. I wish I knew who did. I wish I could give you that. All I can give you is the promise that if you stay, I will do all I can to protect the pack, and if you go, I will tell no one we had this conversation."

"You'd lie for me?" That caught me off guard.

"If Bastian asked, I would tell him. But only him. He'd deserve the truth."

That flared my anger up again, as if he had a right to speak of such things. "All of it?"

He flinched then, eyes closing for a moment before he sighed. "That would be up to you, Kathryn. And what you considered reasonable to share. He's quite in love with you, I'm sure you've noticed."

"He's kind."

"However you wish to say it. Bastian is a good man. If you wanted to tell him all, I wouldn't think you were wrong. Equally, you might want to save his heart from the pain. Knowing what his father did would hurt him. But you will know your own counsel there."

"I don't know if he'd be in love with me if he knew I was a weapon."

"He's a wolf. We are not strangers to wounds."

"Even those done by the pack against their own?"

He nodded, giving a shaky exhale. "Gillian and I are maybe more aware of those than the others. She was worried you would come here wanting vengeance, to hurt Bastian."

"Why would I do that?"

"To hurt us."

I laughed, and it rattled against my teeth like a marble. "You're telling on yourself there, no? I wouldn't hurt a child to get to their parents. I would have thought that was clear when I sent Annabelle running home."

"It was." He looked me over for an inscrutable minute, eyes ticking over me. "Would you hurt one of us directly instead?"

"Never even thought about it." I sat back on the sofa, shaking my head. "Maybe I lack the wolf's instincts. My magic isn't like your wild blood, but no. I never thought about coming and doing something about it. I hated you, hated you lots, but I wouldn't have sought to harm you. You all had families. There was only me left alone, trying to figure out what I was after she died."

"Did you?"

"I'm untrained."

"You did something to Joshua in the woods. He looked almost afraid."

"I don't think he expected me to headbutt him, to be fair."

"Kathryn." He tried to be stern.

"Did Seb tell you about the flames I have?" I held my hands out in front of me, fingers splayed. "He saw them when I was attacked at home. They're not automatic, it's usually fear that does it. They're blue, the flames, like my fathers. More instinctual than his, I really should train them in better, but when you run a bookshop, it's harder. So much paper. There was no harm in Josh knowing I was a witch. A bit of fear might do them good, if they're a threat. And Seb thinks they are."

"Quite right." Victor nodded, looking away from me to the window. "I am sorry about what we did to you. How your magic was… maimed. You must know, Karl loved you so much. He would have thought it was better that you could defend yourself. That it wa necessary. Our interference with that w unreasonable."

"You wanted something powerful. Sponta ous manifestation is certainly that. I can't do the th my father did for the rituals, but I can at least prot thers with that."

"Rituals?"

"The blessings and the fertility rites. He never told me much, what father would? But I know that is lacking."

Victor's lips pinched together, all colour rushing out of the thin line it created. "I'm going to say something you might not like, Kathryn. Would you prefer it now, or after the ceremony?"

A thrill went through my chest at the seriousness of his face, a different grimness than that of his stilted apologies. "Now. I still have time to run, as you say."

"Quiet. Your father wasn't a ritual practitioner for us. He did some spell work, but he didn't undertake blessings. What he did was to accompany us on certain jobs. Pack work where we needed additional firepower."

The words crested like a wave, washing over me in a chilling crash. "He was a weapon, too?"

"Yes. His firepower was very literal, like yours."

"At least we have that in common, then." I closed my eyes, shaking my head. "That's why Seb wasn't worried about my not being able to do the rites. They 'on't exist."

"Not anymore, certainly. They may have once. And B ian would never take you on such a job. Not that we dc any anymore, he has refocused on mostly legal ave s. What work is illicit is safe, body guarding and tran , the usual things."

a reformer." Taking a deep breath, I opened my ey in. I would not fall apart in front of Victor.

Not on my wedding day. At least Seb and I were both going in with secrets. We were on equal fucking footing there.

"You could say that."

"I've taken up enough of your morning, Victor. You'll have your own preparations to make for the day. Thank you for listening to me."

He leaned in, holding a hand up. "I don't want you to feel you have to rush off. What I told you must be shocking."

"More shocking than the fact my father used me as an experiment? Hardly. He did bad things to other people too. Maybe that should be a comfort." I stood up, brushing my skirt off.

Victor stood, taking my hands. "He did love you very much. This was a gift. He talked about it like in a fairy tale; a witch that could spin silver and throw fire. Who could calm the beast's heart with a word. It was a great wish, but we hurt you."

"Thank you for your time. I'll see you at the ceremony." I pulled my hands away, going to the door.

"I'll see you there. Unless I don't, in which case I wish you well."

"I wouldn't do that to Seb." I left before I could spit anything else at him, my eyes burning, but I blinked any tears away. We had a show to put on.

CHAPTER 23

I holed up in my room when I got back to the house, listening to the sound of Seb setting up for the day. He would be getting ready here, so I'd risk seeing him at some point when I went to Marie's, but I could try to time it with him being busy.

I brooded over Victor's words as I sat in the room, twisting my hair in and out of a braid, checking the wounds on my chest, examining the bruising on my neck in the mirror. There were lots of little things I could do rather than have a fight with him. I just had to make them last long enough.

My efforts were shattered when he knocked on my door, part way through me examining how much of the wound at my shoulder would show.

"Kat, you okay?"

I took a deep breath, looking at my reflection as I answered. It would not do to fight. We could talk later. "Yes, getting ready to go."

"I had something I wanted to give you before you head off."

I closed my eyes, breathing in as deep as I could, holding it for a few beats. "Hold on a second. I'm not decent."

I shed the towel I'd been using in place of risking blood on my dress, tugging on a t-shirt before I went to the door.

Seb stood to attention, fiddling with a small black bag held between both palms. "Can I come in?"

"It's your house, of course you can."

He pulled up, brows furrowing. "You sure you're alright?"

"Wedding jitters."

"If you say so, beautiful. I wanted to give you something before the ceremony. It's not exactly what I wanted, but it's the best I could do on short notice. I'll get you something proper later on, okay?" He was almost sweating, his brows down together like he was delivering terrible news.

"Seb, calm down. What is it?"

"Here." He handed me the bag, hands sinking into his pockets after he did. "Be careful when you open it."

"Alright." I undid the tie at the top, feeling along the shape of whatever lay within. Pushing up, the handle of the something became visible, and as I grasped it I pulled out a short silver knife, the blade maybe the length of my index finger and shiny with polishing. It was heavy, balanced in the middle by a thicker bolster that bore the scratches of recent workings, and only one side was sharpened for use, the other flattened like a cooking knife. It was beautiful, clearly made by someone who knew what they were doing, and the leather around the short handle was soft as butter. All my earlier anger at him ran out of me like a stream, the gift such a sign of worry that I couldn't find it in me to spit my venom his way.

"It's silver," he said, watching me examine it. "Full silver, not a coating. I thought it might make you feel safer. And let me relax, knowing you had a proper weapon. A regular knife would work, most times, but if a wolf were to attack you silver will really hurt. It'll get you time to get to me."

I looked up at him, unsure of how to respond. "You got this for me in case they attack the wedding?"

"No, I wanted you to have it. I know I won't be with you all the time, but it's small. You can hide it in a pursue, or on you, if you need to. Oh, and this too." He pulled something out of his back pocket, a folded up black item that he shook out.

"What is that?"

"It's a garter. Not a wedding garter, it's for the knife." He held it up, showing two thick strips of black material with small holding loops on one side. "I know asking you to wear it to the ceremony might seem insane, but would you?"

"Seb, you're going to be standing right next to me."

"I know. But would you?" He bit his lip, face as grim as a ghost.

I shook my head before I took it from him. "Alright. You're lucky I chose an A-line dress. It shouldn't be too obvious. You'd be screwed if I was in that mermaid number."

"Too impractical. You couldn't run." He shook his head.

"You sure you don't want to give me a mace instead of a bouquet?"

"Like the pointed ball?"

"Since you're arming me and all."

He laughed, shaking his head. "Too obvious, even for some of the idiots we'll see today."

"I'm not sure I'd call a silver dagger exactly subtle, but fine. It can come to the wedding. I might even keep it on tonight."

"Thank you. Are you really just nervous?"

I laughed, shrugging. "Mostly that, yeah. We can talk it all through after the ceremony, and the first run. I presume I'm hanging out at the tent while you do that?"

"For the first loop, yes. I'll come back after that. The clearing isn't huge, it won't be long."

"More time for me to eat the food."

"I'll never tell." He winked, taking my hand. "I'll stay out of your way so you can head over, but I'm looking forward to tonight. I know you'll look amazing."

"I will if Marie has anything to do with it." I smiled, squeezing his hand. "Are you really worried about it?"

He sighed like the wind in autumn, those lovely eyes looking anywhere but me. "I'd feel better if we knew what had happened to my dad. Given we don't, and there's someone actively trying to do you harm, I don't feel good about going in without a plan. This is a good start to a plan."

Sweet man. We would still need to have words, but I should have known that guilt would be in his mind. "Okay, I can work with that. But the next time you buy me underwear, you're going to have to make it way more fun to make up for me having this strapped to my leg."

"I'll look forward to it." He tugged me closer, pecking a kiss to my forehead. "Have fun with Marie. See you soon."

~

I left for Marie's not long after, taking the dagger with me as I threw a handful of items into a carry bag. I'd left most things with Marie, including the jewellery, so I only had to bring myself and my recent additions. And my shoes for walking up.

We were part way through doing my hair when a knock sounded at the door, disturbing our gossiping back and forth.

"I'll go," Gillian said.

Marie kept working on my hair as Gillian went to the door, frowning at me as she teased the curls left from my earlier braid into something more recognisable as a style.

"I don't know how you don't go to frizz every time you walk out the door with this. It's so thick!"

I winced. "It involves a lot of conditioners, I promise. Oils too. It drinks anything it can get."

"If you say so girly, I'm going to have to use the least heat I can get away with, and that will not be quick."

"I trust you, do as you must!" I giggled at how serious her face was, brows drawn down low, just like Seb. It was so sweet.

"Girls, we have company. Kathryn, you may want to change slightly before you meet them."

I was sitting in a robe, so I didn't have to disturb my hair any more than necessary once Marie had worked her magic, and I blinked at Gillian mutely for a long minute. "Company?"

"Will Campbell is insisting on a meeting before the ceremony. I knew they were pushing for it, but we all thought they'd drop it. It's more old-fashioned than they usually are. If you pop a wrap dress on, I'm sure it won't cause any trouble with Marie's work."

"Is Josh with him?" Marie scowled, darting out from the living room to grab me something and throw it my way. A light summer dress landed in my hands, dropping edges showing a wrap style. I shed my robe and slid it on, quickly tying the internal fasten and then fixing the external one at my hip. It was too small for me by maybe a size, Marie being shorted than me, but it covered all the necessary.

"No, Victor and Will. Seb's getting ready, and it'll just distress him. As officiator, it's technically Victor's role to broker their attendance, but I think he wants it over with." Gillian's face was pinched, too much tension around her eyes.

I stepped forward, catching her eye. "That's fine. We can do this. Better we make a good impression, even if they're rivals, yeah?"

"It will be useful for the wedding if we get this over with, yes." She glanced back over her shoulder. "It's rude of him to insist so late in the process. Shockingly rude."

"Probably because I head-butted Josh, to be fair. I can see why that would make him difficult."

Gillian almost laughed. "That may have some element of it, yes. Marie, stay by Kat. Even if Victor says otherwise."

Marie nodded, linking our arms together. "No problem."

We left the living room to find Victor and another man, presumably Will Campbell, in the kitchen. Victor had made them coffee, mugs on the counter with steam enough to join the thick silence we walked into.

"Kathryn, thank you for seeing us so late in the day." Victor came forward, giving me a half-hug, and Marie tightened her grip on my elbow. "This is Will

Campbell. He wanted to come to see you personally about the incident in the woods."

"I wanted to clear the air before the big event." Will pushed himself off the counter, stepping closer. He was almost ages with me, maybe into his thirties, with dark, curly hair that sat close to his skull, and the sort of blue-grey eyes that changed with the light. He was slighter than I expected for a wolf, not small but not the same broad shape as Seb or Daniel, and while he was tall, he didn't show it off, his shirt basic and neat.

He held his hand out. "A pleasure to meet you, Kathryn."

I shook his hand with my free one, trying my best not to smile at the way Marie bristled. "And you too. Josh already apologised; I don't consider us to have an issue."

"He admitted he had, but I wanted to make it clear we don't all behave like that. He is over eager in his efforts, sometimes, much as he's a fine second for me. I don't want us to have cause to quarrel on your big day."

"As long as he doesn't choke me again, I'm sure we won't."

He smirked, eyes lingering on the marks at my neck. "If he tries that again, I'll break his wrist myself. I promise you that. It was a poor display."

"Thank you for taking the time to say that. Though I think he did worse to Seb, when they were tussling."

Will shrugged. "What wolves do in a tussle is the way of nature. You're not a wolf."

"No, I'm not. Though I've been around them a long while."

"Kathryn was with the pack long term, before she had to move," Victor said. He steered himself in, reaching across Will to put his cup down on the counter, and I could have hugged him properly this time. Something about Will's amiable smile and lingering eye set my hackles off, despite the cordial nature of his comments.

"I'm glad she's returned. I hope you'll be joining Seb for the negotiations. You seem to have a good head on your shoulders."

"With no offence meant, Will, how would you know that?" I tilted my chin at him, unsure if he was mocking me with the glib comment.

"You've kept Marie here, just in case. Always a pleasure, Marie." He grinned at her, a lazy wolfish thing that she rolled her eyes at. "And you broke Josh's nose as a distraction to let little Annabelle run home. That's got some good guts, but brains too. A bit of blood in the air to draw the focus. I admire someone so direct."

"I'm glad we could speak plainly, then. I'll look forward to seeing you at the ceremony, unless there's anything else you wanted to discuss?"

"Oh, no, I think anything else can wait until after the fun. I don't want to take up your getting ready time. Plus, Victor here needs time to squeeze into his suit."

Will gave Victor a slap on the shoulder and I could have sworn the sound was overloud in the kitchen.

Victor laughed, shaking his head. “I’m glad we could deal with the matter so quickly. I’ll come and collect the members of the pack attending closer to the time. Thank you for your hospitality, ladies.”

“You’re always welcome,” Marie said. It didn’t sound true, but her smile lasted until they’d left the kitchen. “Fucking creeps, the entire pack.”

CHAPTER 24

The walk to the clearing seemed to last forever, even with Marie keeping me cheerful company. My stomach twisted and span, threatening to turn out the light snacks I'd managed while getting ready, and the dagger Seb gave me sat heavy on my leg even before I slipped into my heels.

They had made the space beautiful: the marquee dominated the far end of the clearing, hundreds of fairy lights strung around the entrance in a glowing arch. They were trailed down to create a winding path from one end of the clearing to the opening of the tent, and the branches in the treeline was decked with strips of pale golden lights too, creating a warm glow that still left enough room for the wolves to run underneath later on.

"Daniel worked all night to get them right," Marie said. She passed me my heels, shoving my trainers in an unlocked supply box. "We'll grab them later."

"He's such a sweetie. He made us that den as well."

"That's where half the lights came from. I didn't even know he recognised fairy lights, and he's got miles of them."

"Bodes well for you two." I winked at her and she giggled, batting my shoulder.

"No rush yet. We've other things to do first." Her hand rested on her stomach, the skirt of her dress too loose to show anything, and I nodded.

"Get this one down first, then we can start a new folder off for yours."

"I wanted you to have something. Wait a sec." She dug into the box as I fixed the slingback on my heels, setting the elastic in a straight line so they didn't rub as I walked.

She stood, handing me a bouquet of deep blue roses, almost black, and when I took the bundle, I felt the petals were material.

"They're an old prop, from a play I was in as a kid. I was this horrible ghost woman." She waved her hand self-consciously. "I saved them, for some reason. I think it was because I could, and I was thinking about the traditions. You need something old and new, borrowed and blue, right?"

"That's what they say."

"So that's three of your options; old, blue, and borrowed. I'll have it back when you're done. And the jewellery is new, so you're all set. I suppose we should have got you a silver coin too, but I think Seb's kind donation covered that side of things."

"Why go for a coin when a knife is an option? Thank you, Marie."

"No problem. I wanted you to have as much good luck as possible. I know we say we make our own, but we've not been very lucky recently and I want this to go well."

A whole family of worriers, it seemed. I leant in and hugged her, even taller than her in my heels, and I cupped her cheek as I pulled back. "You're going to be an awesome sister-in-law."

"Oh, Kitty-Kat, don't say things like that. You'll make me cry!" She pecked a kiss to the heel of my hand, flapping her own at her face to dissuade any tears. "Come on, we have to head in. Folk will be waiting."

"Will they already be sitting down?"

"They'll be rounding up the last stragglers. I'll accompany you to the start of the aisle, then walk behind, like I'm your second. I know there's no one to walk you down, but I'll have your back. Promise."

I near cried at that, squeezing her hand. "Thank you."

"No problem. Let's go knock them dead." She winked, then let out a sharp whistle, which triggered music to start up.

We walked along the lamplight path, still bright despite the dying sunset somewhere behind us, Marie's elbow tight beside mine as we got steadily closer. As we passed underneath the glowing arch, she led me deeper into the tent, behind organised rows of seats with vines or flowers intertwined at the backs of them. It was a sea of green and blue, as wild as the woods and the night sky, and there were precious few empty seats – even my side had filled up with members of the rival pack. I thought I spied Josh down in the front rows in a suit, but I would believe that when I got closer to inspect it.

Marie let go of me as we reached the start of the aisle, and at the end I saw Seb and Daniel stood, whispering to each other. Daniel noticed me first, flashing a bright smile before he elbowed Seb and nodded in my direction.

Seb turned to look as I started walking, his eyes widening as he took me in, and I smiled back at him as I took steady steps closer, timing them with the cheerful march that had started up somewhere. It sounded like actual music, not a quick recording, but I hadn't noticed a band and I was took fixated on watching Seb to check. His eyes held my gaze, the wolf inside clear in the open warmth there, and my heart fluttered.

I reached him, smiling to Victor before I took my place opposite Seb, stealing a glance out to the rows before us. Josh really had gone to the effort of a suit, and Will was sitting beside him, also done up for the occasion, a waistcoat and jacket covering the plain shirt from earlier. A selection of other men sat with them, and a single older woman who had her steely hair done up in a beautiful French bun that shone like a pearl. I'd find out who she was later on. Her smile was kinder than anyone else on my side.

Victor gave a small cough before he spoke, looking over the crowd.

"Thank you for joining us on this promise night. Bastian, leader of the Weir pack and untested son of

John, is joining with Kathryn, witch to the pack and beloved daughter of Sophie and Karl. While Kathryn has been absent from us for some years, and returns without her kin, we welcome her in as one of our own and she joins with us tonight under the full moon. Their promise has borne the test of time, and they have sought each other out in the darkness of grief and loss."

He paused, grasping Seb's shoulder in a small squeeze, before he continued.

"Those who join with the pack do so in trust and knowledge. Trust that our teeth will not encircle their throats, and knowledge that we would spill blood for them. Kathryn, in turn, brings her magic, and Bastian enters this union with the trust that her magic is for the good of the pack, and the knowledge that she will follow him into the night, bound by the moon and the witnessing of their pack mates."

Sweat prickled over my back at the solemn words. I should have told Seb. I should have made sure he knew we weren't lying. He held my gaze, no hint of discomfort at the lines, and I smiled back at him. This would be easier to explain afterwards. Probably.

"We will now have the—"

"I have a slight issue, if I may?" Will Campbell had stood up, cracking his neck as he did, the gasps from the other side of the aisle loud and angry.

"The fuck are you playing at, Will?" Marie was up on her feet, Gillian standing to tug her back down.

"What is the meaning of this?" Victor glowered at the man, no pretence of cordiality, and stepped between Seb and me.

"We've heard some beautiful words about the love of the couple, and I have no doubt of the truth of that. You can see it plain as day on their faces." Will turned to look at the gathered crowd, pointing at us. "But we have seen nothing of her magic, since she arrived with the pack even. Isn't one of the traditions that a magic user evidences their worth?"

"An ancient tradition, not invoked for decades," Victor said. "If you wanted a demonstration, you should have called for one well before the ceremony!"

"What's the play here?" Seb said, a low growl in his voice. I reached around Victor to tap Seb's wrist, squeezing a little.

"I simply think it's appropriate that we see the truth. Kat, if I may call you that, is beautiful, simply stunning in that dress, but while her ethereal beauty is charming, that's not the same as actual talent."

The growl behind me could have been Seb or Marie, I couldn't tell which. There was only the rushing sound of blood in my ears, and the heat of my fury creeping up my neck in an angry flush.

"You should have asked for one earlier, Will. I'd have pulled a rabbit out of a hat for you."

He sucked air through his teeth as if considering the offer. "That's an old trick."

"I bet you're very familiar with those." I smirked at him, shaking my head. "Okay, you want to see what I can do, get one of your men to attack me."

He blinked at me. "Pardon?"

"Kathryn, absolutely not!" Victor grabbed my elbow, turning me. "That's much too dangerous."

I shook him off, my anger building steam. "It's fine. Josh, you had your hands on me earlier. Want another shot? I'll even arm you. Here."

I bent down to reach under my skirt, loosening the dagger before I pulled it free. I tossed it to Josh, still sat down and blinking furiously, and he caught it as it slapped into his chest. "You were armed?"

"Of course I was." I winked at Seb. "Now come on, on your feet and take a swing at me."

"Boss, nah, are we really?" Josh grabbed Will's jacket sleeve and Will shook him off, a wide grin tugging at his face.

"You're inviting one of my men to hurt you? I want this clear for any witnesses."

"Like hell." Seb stepped forward, and I leaned in to peck a kiss on his cheek, one hand on his chest.

"Trust me."

"Josh, try to stab her." Will's comment interrupted any chance I had at convincing Seb, so I stepped closer to the front row, watching Josh force himself up like a scolded child. Gone was the bluster of the morning, his shoulders slumped. The woman at the end of their row crossed herself, lips pinched together as she looked at me.

Josh came within a few steps of me, wrinkling his nose before he sighed. "Kat, I don't know about this. I much preferred the back and forth of earlier, if I'm honest, and getting a few good hits in on him."

"Shut up and get on with it." I sneered, angling to ignite some of the bravado from before, and a laugh shook out of him like a loose tooth.

"Well, who am I to refuse a lady? If you say so." He tossed the knife up with a flourish, grabbing it out of the air so the blade ran out of the end of his palm, and lunging forward. He was so fast, my hands up in front of me to ward off the knife like that would help, eyes screwed shut.

Arms closed around me from behind, a hot chest at my back, and the someone was screaming. Peeking my eyes open, I found Seb's arms around me, his head tucked into my neck, and Josh flapping his arms around as blue fire ate hungrily up his sleeves.

"You knew I was going to be safe," I whispered.

"I couldn't watch him do that." He pecked a kiss on my neck. "Also, my jacket's on fire. I'll have to do the rest of the ceremony in shirt sleeves."

"I hate to interrupt this sweet moment, however, Kat, would you mind putting my man out?" Will appeared before us, pointing to Josh, who had gone to the ground and was rolling on the wooden floor covering set out for the chairs.

"You can stamp it down," I said. "He has the right idea. Stop, drop, and roll."

"We'll have words about this, Will." Seb stepped away.

Victor pushed past us, shedding his own jacket and taking Seb's too, before he helped put Josh out. Someone else from the pack ushered Josh away, through the archway - probably to get first aid, but I was distracted getting my knife back to keep track. It was much too hot to set against my thigh again, so I nudged it to beside my foot, cooling in the grass.

"Can we consider this challenge answered, Will?" Victor asked as he returned.

Will hummed, gripping his chin. "Not quite. That was a passive magic, if I'm not mistaken. It had to be induced by an attack."

"Yes. It's a protective expression of magic," I said.

"Then that could be anyone's magic. Your late father worked for the pack. It could be a dying blessing from him. You were in the pack when he was killed, weren't you, Kat?"

My blood fizzed, the smile on my lips somewhere between a snarl and a grimace. Never mind him breaking Josh's wrists, I was going to take his throat with no need to change under the moon. "He died in service to the pack, yes. Though I think you have a poor understanding of magic if you think something like that would still work eleven years later."

"Can you do anything else? Anything to prove the magic is yours?" Will stepped closer, eyes ticking over my form. "Just so we know everything's as it should be."

I nodded to the way Josh had disappeared. "I'm a witch, not a magician, but I don't think your second thinks things are how they should be."

"Stop this, now. You've had a demonstration." Victor made to steer Will away, but Will shook Victor's hand off.

He turned to the other wolves, shouting. "She doesn't smell of magic. I demand to see evidence of her powers."

"Fine." I grabbed the bouquet Marie had loaned me, dropped in the scrum, and plucked one rose free. I brought the material bloom to my lips, closing my eyes to press a kiss to the false petals, and pushed my will into the shape of it. I imagined the curve and sway of each fold, the weight of the stem in my hand, the bumps and thrusts of each false thorn, and pulled all my focus in until it turned cold and metallic in my grasp. The fibres wove together and changed with a small hiss, the lingering scent of burning metal overtaking the burning material behind us.

I straightened my arm out, holding the silver rose high so it could catch the many little lights making the whole place glow.

"What the fuck?" That was Daniel, as was the grunt that followed from someone elbowing him. Seb, I expected.

Will blinked up at the flower, eyes slowly lowering to stare at me. I brought the flower back down, swinging it around to press at his throat. His back straightened, tongue slipping out to lick his lower lip.

"Spontaneous manifestation of silver, to go along with the fire. I trust that's enough of a demonstration for you?" He swallowed, and I pushed the sharp edges a little harder, spite and venom warring in the tremble at my wrist. "*Speak.*"

He held his hands up, ducking his head. "I stand corrected. Truly, you have your magic, and you are more than a better match for Seb. He's a lucky man to have such a talented wife."

"Thank you." I took the rose from his neck, threading it back into the bundle. The silver would dissipate in a few hours, draining away like frost melting in the sun, but there was no reason for them to know that.

"The challenge having been met, I call this ceremony to order once more." Victor took up his spot at the end of the aisle, drawing Seb and me back towards him. "I trust there are no further challenges?"

"She has the blessing of our pack." All heads turned to the older woman with the Campbells, her pinched lips now a smile. "She's more than strong enough. No challenge from us."

"Thank you, Irene." Victor nodded her way. "In that case, I call upon those here to mark this night as the first of the joining between Bastian and Kathryn. May their joining bring prosperity to the pack, and may those that can do so join with us for a run into the woods to revel in the blessings of the moon."

Seb leaned forward, catching my cheek in one broad palm to bring me in for a kiss. Whoops and claps went up, louder on his side than mine, though some of the Campbells had the decency to shout for us, and as we parted, I saw Will clapping along with the rest.

Seb turned to the crowd, waving the hand that was not holding me. "I plan to kiss my wife again, then I will join with you for the run. A moment of your indulgence."

"Aye, right!" Someone called, and I was grateful when Seb grabbed my wrist to pull us out of the back of the tent, towards a smaller one I had to presume was set up for privacy for the change.

CHAPTER 25

The tent was larger than I expected, for a privacy point, easily enough space for three or four people, and as we entered, we nearly bumped into a beaten-up couch at one side, covered in blankets and cushions. A small pile of books sat on a pop-up fishing table too, battered old copies of things you'd see accumulating dust on people's bookshelves.

"What is this?" I asked.

Seb glanced at the couch, sighing. "I had them put at tent up for you to wait in, in case someone tried anything. Which they did. Kat, what the hell was that?"

"You tell me, I don't know werewolf wedding rules, Seb. I didn't get the memo that they could challenge you in the ceremony! All your talk about attacks and you didn't mention this part?"

"You know that's not what I'm talking about." He dropped my hand, crossing his arms as he frowned at me. "You said you didn't have magic."

I tilted my chin at him, crossing my arms in turn. "I said I was untrained, and I am. No one ever taught me how to manage my magic. My mother didn't have the talent and my father was dead!" I tried to keep my voice down, bristling with my anger but not wanting to start a fight when everyone was gathered nearby.

"So how the fuck did you turn a rose into silver, then?" He stalked away from me, kicking the couch, and my chest tightened at the loud thud it made. That would have hurt. It would hurt to run on too, when he had to change.

"It's only temporary, look." I threw the rose at him, the stem already returning to plastic, though the petals glinted and there was a solid 'thump' as it hit his chest. "If it were permanent, I'd be a damn sight richer than running a bookshop, wouldn't I? I had to navigate this on my own, I barely know what I can do or if it's right or wrong. I just know what I can do so far."

He tossed the rose onto the sofa, jaw working before he spoke. "You lied to me."

"I did not. I told you I wasn't taught. That's true. And you have precious little room to get sensitive about lying."

He pulled up, his shoulders dropping. "What do you mean?"

"The rituals I was so worried about? How I agonised over not being able to help, because I couldn't do the things the pack needed? You neglected to mention they don't fucking exist."

"Kat, I…" He trailed off, coming closer. Sighing, I turned half away from him, watching the door of the tent but not putting my back to him. I was hot with anger, all the way to my bones, but we had appearances to keep up. "I didn't know what to say. If your mother hadn't told you, I thought there was a reason. That she wanted you to think well of your dad."

I laughed, a shrill sound that bounced back at me from the canvas. "For being muscle for the pack? A living weapon, firepower for the jobs. He did worse things than that; you don't even know."

"What do you mean, beautiful?" He caught my elbow, turning me to look at him. I let him, let myself see that suddenly earnest gaze again.

"It's a long story. Which I'm not even inclined to tell you, given you already know more than me."

"I didn't want to risk you. For the pack to see you as a weapon." I hissed air through my teeth in a sharp inhale, dropping my gaze from him like he'd slapped my face. He meant well. I knew he would, somewhere between my anger and my fear, but I couldn't look at him. Of course they would see me as a weapon, until they realised what else I could do, then they'd see me as an awful lot worse. Wolves never welcomed a threat. The silence stretched between us for a long minute.

"What else have you been lying about?" I asked eventually.

He cleared his throat. "There were a couple of things. If you really want me to tell you."

"Yes, Seb, I really do." I glanced back up at him, hated myself for the stricken look on his face. "We're married now, so may as well get it out of the way, no?"

"Well, we haven't filed the paperwork yet…"

I shook my head at his weak attempt at a joke. "You're lucky I left the dagger in there."

"And I didn't like that you armed Josh, for one thing."

"I needed it to be a real fright. The flames need genuine fear."

"Effective as that may be, seeing you stabbed with a knife I gave you would have been intolerable."

I scowled at him. "I'll pass him a steak knife should the need ever arise again, then. Talk."

"Can we sit down?"

"No. Stop stalling and tell me!" I turned to face him fully, pulling at the reigns of my restraint not to shove him in the chest.

"I'm worried you'll hate me."

"Seb." I shook my head at him, hands up to cover my mouth before falling down again. Hopefully, the lipstick smudges would look like kissing. "Seb, I swear to whatever listens up there if you don't spit it out, I'm going to go for your throat myself. I won't hate you." Probably.

"We could have waited until the next full moon." He said it in a rush, like getting it out would make it disappear between us. I blinked at him, mind scrabbling.

"We what?"

"For the ceremony. We could have waited until the next full moon. Given my father's death was by violence, there would have been leeway." He grabbed my hands, squeezing them between his own large palms. They were warm, even in the muggy heat of the evening. "But I was so scared you'd be at risk, and then with the attack on your house, then your shop, I knew it wasn't safe for you to be left out in the cold."

I stewed in that thought for a long second, working my tongue against the roof of my mouth before I spoke. "So instead of telling me you lied about shame and pain in the pack."

"It seemed too late to tell you once you were here. Once we were friendlier." He cupped my cheek, and I shook his hand off, fit to bite if he tried to touch me again.

"You guilt tripped me about both of our dead parents! You could have told me the truth."

"I know. I'm sorry, Kat. When you got hurt at your house, all I could see was my dad. The blood." He tapped his chest, fisting his hand into his shirt. "There's so much damage after a shotgun blast."

Ah, shit. Of course, that's what he saw when I'd been cut. I'd been so wrapped up in fear I didn't think of anything but the grief, there was bound to be some shock as well. He'd seen his dad dead.

"Is there anything else?" I asked. "That you've not been honest about?"

"I knew I wanted to marry you at fifteen. It wasn't just the promise. I don't know if I've exactly lied about that, but I want to be clear."

"Right." But he never came to see me, or find me out, until his dad died. "Well, I have a couple, too."

"Couple?"

"Of lies. First, surprise, I really am magic." I held my arms out, shaking my open palms in a sad 'tah-dah'. "Self-taught, so not very good, but yeah. Magic. Second, part of that—"

A scream ripped through the humid air, human and female, and we barely glanced at each other as we ran back into the main tent.

There was a fighting scrum at the front benches. Gillian and Irene stood off to one side, hugging each other like they were stricken, several of the men facing up so their foreheads near touched, glinting teeth bared.

In the aisle Daniel and Josh were tussling, down on the ground trading blows and snarls as if they would slip into the wild at the first drop, ready to tear chunks from one another, and further up the path Will Campbell stood with one hand on Marie's throat, her back pressed to his chest.

"Marie!" I screamed, the sound squeezing out of me as I folded down into myself, a dreadful chill of fear rushing through my stomach. The scrum turned to us, even the fight on the floor stalling, and I scrabbled forward. Seb grabbed my arm, linking our elbows, only pausing in his stalk forward to let me grab my little knife.

"What the hell is this?" Seb shouted, muscling between the posturing men to get to Daniel and Josh.

"We show you hospitality and you start a fight at my wedding, Will?"

"I laid no hand, she slapped me."

"You challenged incorrectly! If you'd needed an example, you could have done it this afternoon, you little dickhead." Marie struggled in his grip and his fingers tightened at her throat, stilling her. It was a pack thing for them, then, the choking.

"Get your hands off her." Daniel made to stand, lunging forward, but even burned Josh had hold of him, yanking Daniel back down and twisting on top of him.

"Your second also threatened me, but Josh is taking care of that," Will said. "While my challenge was misplaced, Kat answered it admirably. As such, there's no aggression on our side. You struck first."

"You're lucky I didn't wait until the run and bite your eyes out, you weasel faced prick." Marie's face was turning red - water in her eyes - and my stomach fluttered. This wasn't safe.

"Such a mouth on you. This is why we need to have a proper negotiation, not some pot-shot attempt at peace." Will laughed, looking back up to Seb. "Come to table, at my pack space, two hours from now. I'll take her with me."

He made to turn with Marie and I shot forward, dropping Seb's arm. "No, take me!"

Will paused, as did the tussling between Josh and Daniel, as all eyes came to me.

"Pardon?" Will asked.

"Take me instead. I'm his favourite, and taking a wolf is bad faith negotiation. I can't turn with the moon, so you know I won't hurt one of you." Josh cleared his throat, and I scowled at him. "Shut it, he asked for a demonstration."

"Kat, what are you doing?" Seb was at my side, tugging my elbow. "This is crazy. We can't let them leave with either of you."

"Your entire pack is here. Kids, Seb. We can't have bloodshed."

"Are you freely offering yourself for us, little witch?" Will walked closer, dragging Marie with him. She shook her head frantically, but her face was still turning crimson, and all I could think of was her secret news.

"For the negotiation only, yes. I'll be your hostage, not her."

"Kat, no!" Seb near shouted, pulling me close to his chest, his arms caging me against him. "Babygirl, this is too much. You can't do this."

"I have to."

His grip tightened on my arm, panic clear in the pant of his breath. "Beautiful, don't do something so stupid."

"Blood and peaches," I said, twisting to look at him. His eyes widened, and I tipped my head to Marie a little. "Blood and peaches. Yeah?"

He looked between Marie and me, his jaw working. "Yeah?"

"Yeah. So it has to be me. Let me." I pushed Seb away, hopping over the tangle of legs that were still Josh and Daniel.

"Kat, what are you doing?" Daniel said, and I ignored him, much as it hurt me to, keeping my eyes on Marie.

Will only let go of her when I was standing before them, and I scooped her into a desperate hug as she collapsed into gulping breaths. "It's okay, you're alright."

"Kat, no, no, you can't go with them." She gripped onto my arms, shaking her head. "You can't do this. We just got you back."

"I'll be back again. There's no point killing a good hostage, is there, Will?"

He inclined his head. "Not too early, at least."

Marie sobbed, and I held her closer, stroking her hair. "I'll be right back. You just be okay, alright? Daniel, come on." I patted Marie's back, waving him closer with the same hand. Josh let him up, and I had to push Marie into him as she screamed again.

"Quite the show. Are you that desperate to leave?" Will was at my back, his hand on my shoulder, and I straightened my spine rather than look at him.

"I didn't need your man to have another excuse to beat a woman. I'm impressed the bruising on his nose isn't out yet."

"Irene helped with that. She has magic, too. You'll come quietly?"

I watched Daniel drag Marie back towards the waiting pack, more sobbing than screaming now, and my heart wavered as I saw Seb step in to help. "Yeah, I will."

"Good girl. I knew you had more sense in you than that pup."

"Enough!" The shout came from Irene, who embraced Gillian before they separated. She looked around the gathered men, before settling her gaze on Seb. "We will return to our space. Come in two hours, as Will has said. No harm will befall your mate before then. She will be welcome in my den, as a fellow practitioner."

Seb nodded, moving away to let her pass as she walked towards Will and me, and the other Campbell pack members filed in behind her.

"I will see you shortly, Seb," Will called. He offered me his hand, and I shook my head, holding a fist above my heart for a moment as I looked at Seb. He nodded, an arm still around Marie's sobbing form, and I turned away before I cried as well.

CHAPTER 26

The walk to the Campbells was actually only to their cars, sat waiting in a parking space I had to presume had uses other than the wild running. My feet ached by the time we got to the cluster of vehicles, but I'd be damned if I was going to show them any weakness. I'd waited tables in heels: this was nothing.

They steered me into a large black car, the back seat broad enough to seat four, though just Will and I took up a spot. I tucked myself into the far door, leaving as much space as I could. Josh took up the driver's seat, and Irene the passenger's side, eyes on the fat orb of the moon that was creeping out of the edges of the horizon, not yet high enough to give proper light.

"We should get back before the night if full. The change can only be delayed so long," Irene said.

"We know. It's itching under my skin already," Josh said.

"Probably the burns," I muttered.

"I doubt they'll help. Though poor Josh has had the rough edge of your mercy twice recently, I would be wary of antagonising him." Will leaned closer, and I held a hand up, palm flat out towards him to keep him at bay.

"He had hands on me, and you made apologies for him. Spare me."

"I intend to. I don't mean any harm to befall you in our company, Kat."

I scoffed. "Good to know."

"However, if you try to run, we will subdue you," he continued.

"I walked out with you, save the scare tactics." I shook my head at him, looking back out at the passing trees. "You know I survived a pack fifteen years before we left. I know how this shit goes."

"Is that why you volunteered yourself, a moon sickness over the wolves?" Will stroked my arm, coaxing, ever so soft. I near hissed at him, wishing I could pour myself out of the window rather than put up with this theatre - there was no crowd to entertain here, no pack to impress.

"That's because of the pups," Irene said.

We all looked at her, and I kicked the back of Josh's seat when he continued to stare. "Eyes on the road!"

"She's pregnant?" Will asked.

"Marie, yes. You can smell it on her." Irene took a wistful sigh, smiling like a pleased auntie. "It's like caramelised apples in the summer's turning. Is that what you get too, Kathryn?"

I sank back in my seat. "Peaches, for me. Peaches and blood."

Will laughed, scratching his chin, and a brief smile tugged at his lips. "That's why Seb handed you over. Did he know beforehand?"

"No, she was saving the news for after the wedding. I told him. That's why he let me go. Probably the shock as much as anything else."

Will looked at me again. "And you worried we'd be monsters to her?"

Heat flashed at my temples, an itch of temper I knew better than to let out. "You were choking her and the risk to the baby was too high. I didn't care if you knew or not. It was within my power to avoid the worst, so I did."

"Such a fearsome little thing. No wonder Seb's besotted."

"All the better for whatever you're after, no?" I glanced high enough to meet his eyes, quicksilver bright despite the gloom of the car interior. I didn't like a bit of this, from not being told they had a magic user to the satisfied way Will was watching me, but there were certain dynamics in a negotiation. I knew how those worked.

Will shrugged, the action ruffling his shirt ever so slightly within his jacket, a little fraying at the edges of his careful posturing. "I suspect his pregnant sister would only be a very close second, but I'd not destroy a babe in the womb."

"A poor bargaining chip, then. You have to be willing to burn the hand for the gamble to really be worth it, and Seb knows that. So I'm better."

"Anyone would think you'd done this sort of thing before." He grinned at me, seeming to enjoy this, and I hated him for it in some distant, far-off way. Too like the old times. But there was no time for old hate when there was present danger.

"They promised me off at fifteen. Do you really think I'd be entirely blind?"

Will hummed in thought, shaking his head a little. "No, I think that would be a mistake."

"Good. What did you do to Victor, by the way? I didn't see him on the floor."

Will's eyebrows popped up, his head tilting to one side. "He ran off not long after Marie launched herself at me. I assumed he was going to get you and Seb, given you came barrelling back in so swiftly. You were rather animated."

"You made her scream."

Will nodded. "That was a shallow strike, all for show. She'd slapped me in front of my men. I had to show strength."

"Whatever you say." I huffed air, shaking my head at him. I had no time for this sort of back-and-forth bullshit, but there was little else for me to do while trapped in the car.

"He went off to get a gun," Josh said from the front seat.

I perked up, leaning forward to see if I could catch his eyes in the mirror. "What?"

"I saw him stashing one this morning, a shotgun and box of shells in one of the supply boxes."

"You failed to include that in your report," Will said. I caught the scowl he was shooting at Josh, tucking that away for future use.

"I thought he was going to come after me with it, given it was his girl I was teasing." Josh shrugged, flexing his hands on the wheel. They were healing, the pull of the moon was good for wolves that way. "Once I knew he wasn't, he was stashing it, it didn't seem that important. We'd overpower them anyway if they tried anything, and it wasn't silver shots."

"Quite the insurance for the wedding." I laughed, my shoulders shaking under the weight of the beautiful topper. "He trusted you enough to bring you into Marie's house, but not enough to stop old habits. What a *resounding* endorsement for you, Will."

"Old habits?" Will peered at me.

"You know what they used to do, before they got old and Seb's influence came in. You must know the stories."

Will hummed again. "I know the pack is muscle for hire. That's well documented."

"Oh yeah, and the rest." I twisted in my corner to look at him, the cold leather of the seat squeaking slightly under my weight. "The Weir's weren't just the usual drug runners and heavy hitters. They sank bodies. They were the firepower you wanted when you rolled into somewhere new and wanted to reduce the numbers. A bloody smear of talent, taking out whoever they were paid to make vanish. My father, he was their magic side of it. If you think my flame's bad, you should have seen what he could do with it. Fear might rule mine, but the spite in that man's hands? The way he could make it dance, ensuring it hurt the most." I sighed, shaking my head. It was a yarn and a spin, an extension of what Victor had revealed this morning, though I had no way to know if it was a lie. My father had done wicked things to me. There was no guarantee he hadn't done worse to others. "We heard the screaming for days, sometimes."

"They let you be around it?"

"Rarely, but mistakes happen. Children see things." I'd done a lot more than see. I was a living testament to his will, his fear, all those things that had been painful and true. "We always knew that was why he was killed, that someone wanted to snuff out what he'd done. Limit the risk. And you brought that up. Oh, that was a mistake. You're lucky I have such a good grip on myself now. If you'd tried that when my mother had died, you'd have been up like a pack of matches."

He was quiet for a long time, only the sound of my speeding breath keeping me company in the dark. My heart was unruly, racing along the adrenaline of the lies and the fear and the desperate yearning I had to sink my thumbs into Will Campbell's eyes despite the fact he was being carefully quiet with me.

Irene broke the silence. "You loved him, despite all that. I can hear it."

"He was my father. Bastard or not, of course I did."

"Wise enough words." She nodded to herself.

"Who are you, by the way? I got your name, but I don't know your connection to the pack. Excuse my ignorance."

"I'm the witch for the Campbell pack. I'm related to Will's mother, who was married to the last leader, previously."

"Previously?" I repeated.

"My mother left him before I was born, though stayed with the pack. As such, I'm not legitimate, but as you say." Will grinned at me, the wolf clear in his eyes. "Bastard or not, my father loved me."

"So, you and Seb are the same. Dead fathers and a pack to lead."

"I have the benefit of age on him, and he the benefit of legitimacy. Until your appearance, I suspected that was the only advantage, and that's not a hard one to break."

I laughed, loud in the small space, shaking my head at him. "You mean to take their pack on? Good luck."

"We have fewer men, yes, but we're not soft. Please don't mistake my civility for an unwillingness to shed blood."

Oh, fuck him, as if that would mean anything to me right now. "I wouldn't dream of it. I saw your hand on Marie's throat, I don't think you're soft. The pack *loves* Seb. Not because he's John's kid, or because he goes swinging his dick around, but because he cares. He knows who they all are, he takes care of them, and he takes care of the new recruits, too. He's a leader."

"And yet you walked off from him, in front of them, no less."

"I've left the pack once and come back again. One more time won't worry them." I crossed my arms, taking a deep breath. "Seb only brought me back so quickly because of the attacks. Your doing, I take it?"

"I don't know what you're talking about." Will leaned forward, catching my eye.

I levelled him a look, my patience too thin to keep the back and forth up. "Really? Your boy there has his hands around my throat first meeting, and you expect me to believe that?"

"I said sorry," Josh said. He sounded like he had at the ceremony, the edge of doubt lingering, tingeing his words.

"If I wanted to attack you, there would be no attempts. I'm an excellent hunter," Will said. "And I knew nothing of you, other than what they disclosed in the negotiations, Seb and Victor, before today."

"Right, that's why you came sniffing around this afternoon. You just wanted to get a look at me?"

He took a hold of my hand, brows down low. "I'm being serious. I have sent no men after you. While we still work in the same areas the Weir's used to, if I wanted you harmed, I would have done so properly, with warning to the pack and after meeting you to evaluate you. We don't attack underhandedly."

"Just other things? Your challenge was out of line."

"I was told you had no magic."

"Well, that's a fucking lie. Did you not speak to your own second?" Josh made a strangled noise, somewhere between a yelp and a cough, and I could have sworn his eyes widened in the rear-view mirror. "Oh shit, you didn't, did you?"

"Josh?" Will asked, voice like ice about to crack.

"I-I don't know. I don't know anything about what she's saying."

I chuckled to myself, shaking my head. "Should have had your own counsel. Josh got a front-row seat to my magic before."

"There was none of that flame shit. She was mostly mouthy," Josh said.

"Mostly," I agreed, crossing my arms. "He's right. I didn't use magic to break his nose. Good healing on that one, though. I must ask you for tips about that later on Irene. I've never been able to do healing with mine."

Will gripped my hand tighter. "Do I need to worry about you doing something stupid, Kat? I'd hope you were more sensible than that."

I smiled to myself, glancing over at him as he leaned in close, his seatbelt discarded to crowd me in. "I'm achingly sensible, Will. Don't you worry."

He sat back, nostrils flaring at the use of his name, clearly not satisfied, and I turned my eyes back out to the darkness. We'd been travelling for about forty minutes, we had to almost be there. Given they shared the running woods, this was a very long way to come.

"I'm pleased. I want to have a sensible conversation with you, in private," Will said.

I shook my head at him. "I can't negotiate for the pack. That will have to be Seb."

"It's only for you. An individual proposition."

"She is staying with me, Will," Irene said. She looked over her shoulder, eyes locking with me as she continued. "Kathryn's afforded my hospitality. That's the only way we left without bloodshed."

Will rolled his eyes. "Yes, yes, as you say. But I will speak to her alone, hospitality or no. You can go scry in a mirror or something."

"I much prefer entrails," she said. I didn't know if she was lying.

"Save that for later on, I'll get you fresh ones. I need to get out and have a run," Josh said.

"Fine. As long as you return before the Weir's get here, shift and stretch your legs. I may do the same after we speak." Will turned to me, squeezing my hand. "We'll be there soon. I'll ensure you're comfortable."

I nodded, unable to trust myself to say anything. I might sob or I might spit and neither was good.

CHAPTER 27

The Campbell's space was more like a work yard than a village, the houses smattered here and there with vehicles and large machinery taking up spots before the more neglected buildings. Seb had told me some of the pack moved off, so I presumed theirs were the houses that stood dark and empty now.

Will accompanied me into a large enough property, a comfortable five bedrooms that was done up for company, porch clean and lights on, with Irene and Josh accompanying us. I didn't get to see where the other men went, but the cars all seemed to pull up in the same parking yard in the same way they'd been grouped in the woods.

Will led us into a large front room, half filled with a large TV and some overstuffed leather sofas that sagged slightly but were clearly well used, magazines and gaming consoles dotted around. It felt like there should be kids there, and I wondered if they were running somewhere else given Irene had been the only woman with the wedding party.

"Now, a few housekeeping measures before we go any further. Kat, are you still armed?" Will asked. I nodded. "Give me the knife."

“I’d rather not.”

“I’ll take it from you if I have to.”

I smirked at him, tilting my chin his way. “Try it. I’m sure it will give me a real fright.”

“You don’t need the knife. You have my hospitality. They will not harm you,” Irene said.

“It will also mean you are unarmed at the negotiation. To preserve my good faith in something actually happening.” Will raised his brow at me and I wanted to slap him. The polite act didn’t stop me being aware he was a wolf, smiles or not, and that I’d only volunteered because of his violence on Marie.

I slid a hand under my dress topped and into my bra, throwing the knife sullenly at him. “Fine. Give it me back when I’m leaving.”

“None at your thigh?”

“I didn’t have time to hike my skirt up. There were other things going on. Check if you want to.” I set my foot on one sofa, pulling the material of my dress tight against my leg. The imprint of the holster showed, empty rings crinkling under the pressure, no blade filling the gaps. Will stepped closer, laying his hand on the shape and feeling lightly around the loops. I glowered at him while he did. He could feel my leg up all he liked, I would not back down.

“I’m satisfied that’s the only one.” He pocketed the blade, stepping back. “Now, Josh, you wanted a run.

Feel free to do so, and Irene can speak with Kat. I will join them after I've attended to other matters."

"Like what?" I asked

"There are preparations to be made for a negotiation. Tempting as it would be to set up an ambush and kill whoever they send, that's a poor way to get genuine progress. Subterfuge only has limited benefits between wolves, as I've said."

"Good to know." I brought my leg down, tucking my arms closer. The house wasn't cold, exactly, but the air had a stillness to it like the room didn't like being empty, and I was tired from the sudden uses of magic to check for anything else. I should eat something, to avoid a blood sugar dip, too.

Will noticed my discomfort. "Irene, give her a cardigan when you get to your room. We won't be accused of mistreating her."

"As you wish. Come along with me, will you, Kat?" She nodded to a door at the far side, the paint around the handle marked with smudges from frequent touches. "My room's towards the back and it's well stocked."

"Alright."

I followed her through the door to find us in a long, plain corridor that was studded with doors - the sort you found in hotels where staff would rush between the kitchen and the serving room, or hide carts full of washing from guests.

Irene seemed to sense my looking around, slowing so we walked together. "I live in the servant quarters. Revamped, of course. They had renovated the house a few times, but I insisted they kept this part separate."

"You don't strike me as a servant."

She chuckled, thin lips pressing together. "No. But it serves me well to be separate, so it is useful to keep."

"Good."

We walked in silence for a minute, the shuffle of her flat shoes and the muted impact of my heels – still hurting my feet from the impromptu hike, I should have grabbed my trainers – before she spoke again.

"I knew your father."

"Oh?"

"Many of the practitioners who worked with wolves ran in the same circles. There's only so many who understand what it's like."

"I'm sure I'll find out," I said.

"I hope so. Here we are." She nodded to a light wooden door before us, ash from the colour and grain, and brought a key out from somewhere in her skirt pockets.

"Thank you for the hospitality," I said as she opened the door.

"You deserve equal treatment and respect as one who has learned."

I laughed, a shrill edge to it, as I bit my lip. "Well, I wouldn't go exactly that far. I'm not trained. I self-taught after my father's death."

She nodded. "I suspected."

"Yeah?"

"Your fire is so like his. When you get more comfortable with your power, it will change, become more your own."

I nodded mutely at her, unsure what to say to that. She smiled, flicking lights on to show the room. It was huge, more like a studio than a bedroom, and filled with stacks of books, plants, hanging crystals and charms, the entire space like a wall of stuttering energy. She'd covered the floor in a mish-mash of rugs, no actual sense of a colour as the patterns screamed at one another, and I blinked back the buzz of magic that swept over me, the hairs on my arms standing up.

"This is busy," I said.

She chuckled, nodding to herself. "I have been here a while. I'm maybe more attuned to it than most. Would you like tea?"

"Yes, please. I don't suppose I can convince you to let me go as well?"

"Not until Will has spoken to you, at least, I'm afraid. I fear he is on a wasted venture there, though."

"What do you mean?"

She went slowly to a countertop on one side of the room, plucking up a kettle from somewhere within the scrum of items, taking it over to a sink further back. "Will is a man with long-term views. His vision is always on the horizon. He and Bastian are alike there, though neither would care to admit it."

"Yeah. I had noticed."

"Will is going to ask you to become part of his pack. To choose him instead of Bastian."

"What?" It was half a shriek, the high note of my voice wrung out between shock and anxiety.

"I know, sweet thing, I know. A useless question given what we saw tonight."

"The wedding?"

She turned to look at me, tuning the water off and slowly coming back to turn the kettle on. "That too. Did you not notice with your fire?"

"I set Josh alight, and it caught Seb's jacket as well. He's fine with my fire. It doesn't burn him."

"Just so, yes." She nodded, as if it meant something.

"My fire hurts those who would hurt me. I know Seb wouldn't do that. He can shout off like the rest of them, that's how wolves are. But he's never made me feel unsafe." That had been everything else. The promise, the pack. The number of people dead. Being in enemy territory.

"Ah." She opened her mouth with a wide gasp, shaking her head quickly. "Self-taught, of course. Your fire protects you, yes, but you're thinking too narrow."

"What do you mean?"

"The fire hurts everyone. Everyone but you, and those you love. Your father's didn't hurt your mother. Did yours?"

My stomach tightened a little, a twinge like I might be sick. "I rarely needed it around her. Never, actually."

"So you'd never see the difference. Then I am sorry to say this, instead of it being of them, but your fire accepts Bastian. He's meant to be yours."

"Yes, we were promised."

She chuckled, nodding to herself again. "Yes, you were. Did you ever wonder why?"

"Because my dad was the practitioner for the pack. Everyone knew that. It caused such trouble when we left."

"Sweetheart, I'm sorry to say this to you on such an eventful night, but you're not thinking things through. Here, tea will help."

She passed me a steaming mug, and I accepted it to hold in both hands. It was a thick, short mug, sturdy enough that the heat radiated through it to warm my palms while I blinked at her. "Thank you."

"You're welcome. I will get you a cardigan too, but this first. Have you heard of fated mates?"

"Of course, it's like the wolf's version of a soulmate. Someone you'll always come back to. I heard all about them growing up, like you do with any gaggle of girls."

"Naturally. You grew up with the pack. This is the way of things. But fated mates are not just wolves."

"Yeah they are, it's Prince Charming with fur. The stories are always wolves. Wolves from rival packs, wolves who meet in a war for territory, wolves who are separated somehow. They overcome everything, or if one dies, the other pines away to death. Even the comfort of the pack isn't enough to make up for the missed connection. Very romantic, but equally grim."

"That's the traditional reading, yes. But the reason it's so often presented as two wolves is because wolves write the stories. Like fairy tales always including a human stumbling into magic. We like something of ourselves in our stories."

"You're not a wolf?"

She shook her head. "No. They offered me the bite, but I didn't take it up. Much like your father. And much like your father, I recognise the nature of the fire. Your, and Karl's, fire did not hurt Bastian, because Bastian was bound to you. *For* you. Fated. When Karl saw that, he told John, and they promised you two together. Karl to protect you, because you were bound to be desirable to many others, and John to protect Bastian, because he'd be harmed if you were. As you say, they pine."

I felt like she'd hit me over the head, my mind swirling on the words as if drugged. I'd not even sipped the tea, it wasn't like she'd got me that way, but I nearly staggered at the comments. "That can't be right."

"Why not?"

"Seb is…." I trailed off, swallowing to shake my voice free. "Seb's wonderful. He's a good man, and he's kind. He'd be very easy to love. But he should have a choice about it. He shouldn't be doing it because my broken magic didn't hurt him."

"They've hurt everyone else, have they not?" I nodded. It had been something I was afraid of for a long while. "Then something in you loves him, my dear. And he clearly loves you. That's not a secret from anyone. He looks at you like you're the moon."

"He's going to be a great husband for someone. And I'd like it if it was me. I think I'd like him to choose it, though. I don't want to be someone's duty." Duty was a familiar burden and I wanted to be more than that: I wanted to be loved for myself.

"Then let him choose you. He's his own man, he's capable of making choices for himself and if he didn't want you, he wouldn't have been ready to marry you so quickly. The pack has been worried sick about you, too. I know John tried to bring you back to the pack when Sophie passed on."

I tilted my head at her. "How do you know that?"

"They asked me to approach you. When you confessed to being untrained, and screamed them both out the door. It was possessive, of course, as wolves are. But I think John was genuinely fond of you, not just protecting his son. He worried about you being out on your own."

"You didn't come though."

She laughed, shaking her head. "No, it was none of my business. You were old enough to know your own mind. If I'd known you hadn't been told the circumstances properly, well. That would have been something altogether different. You poor thing, not knowing why you were stumbling around with a hole in your heart."

"I thought it was because of what my dad did to me. My powers aren't…. aren't right." I felt tears hot at my throat, dripping down my cheeks despite my best efforts, and I set the tea down on one of the few available surfaces as I covered my mouth. "Wait, Seb, though, Seb has to be alright. Will he be okay if I die?"

Irene balked part way through taking a sip of tea, shaking her head at me. "Are you planning something heroic? If so, don't, I'll be sure you get back safely. Unless you decide you prefer Will."

"Do we actually die, though, is what I mean? In the stories…"

"I don't think you do." She frowned, considering, her nose wrinkling as she weighed her answer. "If you did, there'd be a lot more wolves pining to death. Every allowing for the smaller part of the population, there's infant mortality rate, especially with wolf pregnancies, natural disasters, the propensity for wolves to fall into criminal activity. I don't know for sure, but I know your magic welcomes him as your own. Try not to die, that'd probably be best."

I frowned at her, wiping my face and picking up the tea again. My make-up would be such a mess. "I've been trying not to. Two attacks, one wolf fight, and one wedding ceremony, and I'm still here."

"Tell me more about the attacks. I heard Will say he didn't do those, and I would believe him. He's not been one to undermine Bastian anything but publicly. Come, sit until Will joins us." She beckoned me further into the room, to a pair of high-backed chairs that sat beside an unlit fireplace. "You can take that cardigan as well, if you like."

I set my tea down, slipping into an oversized cardigan that was hanging off the back of the closest chair. It was a massive thing, shaggy as a sheep with rainbow stripes of colour, each as broad as my palm. I couldn't picture her in it, too lackadaisical for the enthusiastic, if reserved, woman in front of me. "Thank you."

"You're welcome. It was a gift and I never really used it."

Ah, that explained it. "Thank you," I repeated.

"It's fine. Now, two attacks you said?"

"One was at my house. Seb came to pick me up to come back to the pack, and I wanted to talk. We went back to my house, and I was about to cook when a guy, who had obviously been waiting for me to get home, came bursting into the kitchen, knife swinging. He got a good lick in at me, I have a wound here." I ran my fingertip down my sternum.

"And your fire?"

"Set him alight."

"Hm. Concerning. The second?"

"Someone tried to set my shop on fire and left a dead cat knifed into the wall. There was a message about me."

Irene pulled a face, shuffling lower in the chair. "Well, that's certainly not us. Will kills when necessary, but he wouldn't kill an animal unless it was the hunt. He's not wasteful."

"Good to know, I suppose. An appreciation for the cycle."

"He's not a wicked man. In different circumstances, I think he and Bastian might have got along. I'm not sure they could get back to that now, given all that's happened today, but maybe there will be time for that yet. Do the Weirs have any leads?"

"I don't know. Bit distracted with the wedding. I know Seb's investigating his dad's killing and he assumed they were tied together."

"Naturally, but we've naught to do with that. Ask Will yourself. He respected John. It pained him, truly, when John died. Will got some thorough enjoyment of their negotiations, even if it usually involved roaring each other down in the end."

"You sound more like his mum than his aunt," I said.

"I think I've had to be. She died too young. He's careful about it, that's why he mentioned Karl but not Sophie. Let him down as gently as you can, won't you?"

"I'll try to."

"Good. And don't do anything stupid, but that window isn't locked." She nodded to a small door, which may have led to an en suite. "Just in case. I'll go get the door. You stay here."

She stood, leaving her tea, ambling back across the mismatched rugs. The knock sounded as she reached the kettle, and she winked at me over her shoulder. Opening the door revealed Will, suit jacket shed but waistcoat still in place, and his shirtsleeves rolled up to the elbows, so his forearms showed. It was a look.

"That was quick," he said.

"Heard you coming a mile off. Speak to her swiftly. There's not long left before they arrive. I'll give you the room."

"Thank you, Irene." He pressed a kiss to her cheek, standing back so she could leave before he entered. My stomach dropped low when he clicked the lock on the door closed.

CHAPTER 28

"Is that really necessary?" I asked. Locking us in together had a certain look about it, with the best will in the world. While I trusted Irene, there was nothing to say Will would hold the same level of manners.

He turned to me as he pocketed the key. "It's for my peace of mind as much as anything else. If there're any heroics, I would rather know you were safe."

"I'm sure you can give me my dagger back if you're really worried."

"A fair point." He walked over, taking the seat Irene had vacated, and passed the knife back to me.

I took it by the handle, sliding the blade into one of the big pockets on the cardigan. "Anyway, if there was going to be anything like that, Seb would have done it before he left. He'd be too worried about the baby in his sister's belly to do something foolish."

"You really think that?" Will tilted his head at me. It reminded me of being sized up.

"Yes. He'll not risk the safety of the entire pack just to get me back. He'll do as you asked, and we can have a conversation."

Will nodded, face unreadable, and picked up the tea Irene had left. "If you say so. I believe you will have a better read on him than I do. You've known him longer. While our packs aren't strangers, we never much mixed as children."

"You're older than him. You'd be off doing other things."

"That's why we didn't mix, either." He raised his brows at me. Objectively, he would be quite handsome, but all I could see was someone who had set me up at my wedding. Fake or not, that was rude.

"Yeah, I think I would have remembered you."

Will smiled, pale eyes flashing. "I'm certain I would have remembered you."

"Charming as that line is, you watched me get married a scant few hours ago, Will. Unless you have a thing for a certain kind of thing, that's got to be a line."

"Does it?" He took another sip of tea. "You haven't filed the paperwork yet. That won't be until tomorrow, at least. Probably later, Monday morning."

"I'm sure you're not hurting for company." I sipped my tea, drawing the cardigan tighter around me.

"I've had company. I won't pretend otherwise. None with your particular talents, though."

I raised an eyebrow at him. "Your aunt's a witch. You don't need another one."

"I could give you a lot more than Seb. His pack is stronger than ours, truly, but he's a worse negotiator than his father, and we're busy. I could build you a very nice life."

"I don't doubt it. But I've built myself a very nice life, all on my own, and I plan on keeping that. I'm not giving up my shop. Would that be possible with the work you do? It wasn't when I was younger, for my parents. If you're a target, everyone you love is, too."

He grinned, all those white teeth on show, and I could feel the hint of the wolf pushing at the edges as he chuckled. "I'm sorry for bringing your father up. Much as we match on that regard, it was a cheap shot. They had assured us you didn't have magic, and it was an easy way to undermine Seb."

"You could have asked me this afternoon. You didn't need to put Victor to that pantomime if you'd been planning this all along."

Will shrugged. "It was Victor's idea. A way to clear the air. He's been ever so helpful since John died."

Something about the way he said that jarred; snagged in my chest like a bramble thorn. "What do you mean?"

"He's been a thorough negotiator, running back and forth between the camps. Keeping things going in Seb's place. Having an eye on everything, hands on everything. He's damn near stepped into John's boots."

"He was his second."

"As long as I've known either man, yes." Will sipped more tea.

I felt like my chest was going to shatter, something bruised and trembling about to flinch away from pain I knew was coming, but not why. "He told you I didn't have my magic?"

"He and John had consulted Irene previously about you. He reminded me of that. Which was either to humiliate me, which I would not be pleased about, or to undermine Seb, by causing our confrontation."

I sat with that for a long minute, weighing my response in my head. I kept my face as level as I could when I spoke. "He didn't know I had magic. I've always told them I was untrained."

"Self-taught?"

"Yes."

His grin flashed back. "Delightful. Marry me instead."

I shook my head. "I can't. Much as I believe you'd be a lovely man, if I didn't want to sock you one, I'm with Seb for more than the honour of dead men. Did you see him grab me when Josh made to stab me before?"

"I did."

"That fire doesn't hurt him. It's an old magic, love. It's one of the most basic building blocks, but it's what's there. The fire would burn you. And it hurts a lot, as I'm sure Josh told you."

"What a shame. There's no chance of it changing over time?"

I shrugged. "I don't know, really. From what Irene said, I don't think so."

"Of course she noticed that." He smirked, shaking his head. "What a frustration. Well, I seem to have been played."

I spluttered tea, near dropping my cup. "I never gave you any impression…"

"Not you, sweet thing, not you. Much as I would appreciate a chance to change your mind, there's no fun in chasing unwilling prey for mating. I don't want a wife that hates me. No, I appear to have been set up for—"

A shot rang out, loud and angry in the relative quiet of the magic space, and I shoved myself to the ground. It wasn't like there were windows to be shot out; we were fine, but I didn't like guns at the best of times and this was not them, in a strange pack's place, the memory of my father's death fresh as newly spilled blood.

"Are you hurt?" Will was down at my side, hands on my shoulders, as he lifted me up.

"No, it just frightened me. You guys seemed too hands on for guns."

"We use them, but they're all in the lock up currently. I don't have them out except for jobs. We're not exactly the shooting types for a hunt."

"I gathered that." I sat up, wriggling out of his grip. "Is it likely to be one of your men shooting?"

"Not on a full moon, they'd turn. Stay here and keep your knife handy." He patted my shoulder, strangely gentle for a man I'd watched choke Marie earlier, and crossed to the door.

"I could come with you?" I struggled up into standing, ungainly in my heels. "Magic, and all?"

"No. You're under our protection. Stay here." He unlocked the door, slid out, and locked it again by the loud click I heard echo out. Slipping my heels off, I went and tested the door, slapping the wood when I found it locked as expected. I knew he was being sensible, but there was no way in hell I was sitting alone in a room full of magic, waiting for news of someone being shot.

Stalking back over, I put the heels on, no alternative shoes in sight, reviewing my options as I inspected the room. I couldn't pick the lock with my dagger, and I doubted I could pull off breaking the door down, so the window would have to do.

The en suite was massive, much better than any servants' quarters I'd ever seen – not that there had been many - and as promised there was a high, but cracked open, window set in the wall above the toilet. It had two parts, the lower two-thirds one solid, frosted piece, and the upper third propped open on a metal fastener. I faced it up, judging the distance between the frames and the small internal sill, only wide enough for one foot, before looking between the upper part and my hips.

I could fit. Probably. Drop on the other side would be a bit much, but I'd take the heels off before I let go. I might shuck the cardigan off, try to land on it like they taught you to do when escaping a house fire.

It made sense my mother had drilled that into me so often. Bet this wasn't what she had in mind.

Shaking my head, I stood on the porcelain between the back of the toilet seat and the cistern, balancing on my toes as I pushed the window open to peek out. It was cooler than it had been, the heat of the evening broken into proper night, and while I could hear shouting, it wasn't near here.

Fuck it.

I stepped onto the cistern, pushing quickly up so I could launch my arms through the window and pin my weight against the frame. That let me wriggle higher, peering out into the darkness. I should have turned the light off, make my escape less obvious, but time was off the essence if someone was out shooting on a full moon. You didn't show up to a packs house shooting unless you really wanted bloodshed. *Please don't be Seb.*

I shook the thought away. He'd not be that stupid - he'd go by the rules. He wouldn't risk me like that, fight or not.

No one else seemed to be back here, the ground hidden by deep shadows that the meagre bathroom light did little to puncture, and I slid one hand back into the room and grabbed my left shoe, dropping it out into the darkness. It landed with a soft thud, meaning it was likely dirt underneath. That would hurt less than other things.

There wasn't enough room to get myself out and then down like I'd planned. There was no bloody sill on the other side, just a flat drop! Shit. A shout went out, followed by running, and I steeled myself. This was a stupid idea, but I would not sit around to get killed, or have someone else die for stupid traditions.

Reaching back in, I took the other shoe off, dropping it down as well, before I brought my feet up to the thin ledge. I could stand up if I crouched forward, pushing my chest out of the window. The frame bumped against my back; the wood pressing the pearls of the topper into me, but it was too late to wriggle back in and tear it off. I was far enough along that I'd need to go for it.

I didn't look down as I got purchase of the frame underneath my sternum, instead glancing about for any company that might come my way. That was as good a reason as any. I'd never jumped out of a window. It would be fine.

Once I had the heels of my palms in the wood's crook, the hard edges burning as they pressed in, I pushed down, hard, while I shoved up on the balls of my feet. That gave me enough momentum to push myself up, skimming my abdomen and hips through the little space, out into the cool air, and then I was toppling forward and out, down into the dark below.

I span in on myself, the opposite of my namesake, aiming to land on my ass and hips rather than face, bracing in the too brief space between falling and stopping.

The impact radiated from my left shoulder and hip, jarring along my whole spine as I covered my head to shield my face. The pain from landing on one of my heels was sharp enough to signal blood, and I bit my cheek to stifle the cry that tried to escape, my left leg hot and angry from where the shoe heel had scratched an angry line through my dress and into the meat of my thigh. Should have thrown them further off. It was on the outside, at least, and while my dress was no doubt ruined, I could still move my leg around.

I reached around for the other heel as I curled up into sitting, covering my mouth with the cardigan arm as my muscles flared in protest and my back lanced with pain. I had time for that later. Seb could run me another bloody bath, or whatever he wanted, fuss all night long, when I was back with him. And to do that I couldn't stay laid in the dirt here.

CHAPTER 29

The dirt I landed on was hard and easy to force myself up from, a small mercy while everything hurt. I pressed myself back into the wall I'd tumbled down, checking my dagger was still in my pocket – yes. Another mercy.

In front of me there was another building, a small house, no lights shining in the windows. There'd been a large pickup planted on the grass out front, if I'd seen right when we hurried in earlier. Uninhabited, then, or at least not being used tonight. I could limp around to the cars, see if I could get out onto the road and flag Seb down as they approached.

Another shot rang out, close and painfully bouncing back at me from both walls. I covered my mouth as a scream slipped out, small but there, and I held my breath in case anyone came looking.

After counting to ten twice, there was no sound of footsteps coming closer, so I moved. Going for the back garden would mean I could get a view of what was going on between the houses without being in the parking area's open space, and I would make my choices from there. Between the mud and the cardigan, I was a little less obvious that before, no longer a moonlight beacon of white.

I emerged into a spot between two fenced gardens, with little more the scrub grass taking up the yard, and a line of fencing showed a path that ran right along the back of the little gathering of houses. Smaller paths ran up between the detached homes, patchy lights here and there, but it would be enough to run along if I needed to - or hide between one house and the next. This could work.

My burgeoning hope was struck down as I tripped, sprawling over myself in my ungainly flight, and landed hard on the dirt. Looking down, I saw a pair of legs sticking out of one of the smaller paths, the shoes poking past the fence, but that had been enough to catch me. I scrabbled closer, leaning over the length of the body to find Josh shoved tight against the wooden slats, hidden by the dark, and he moaned in pain as I touched him. I yanked my hand back like he scalded it – his chest sodden with blood, his breathing shallow and quick as he writhed under my touch.

"Josh? I need you to wake up. Come on. Josh?" I yanked at him, on my knees to pull at his shoulders, and he moaned again as I dragged him up and slapped at his face. "What happened to you?"

Someone grabbed me from behind, a hand going over my mouth and an arm pinning my own against me as I was pulled up and backwards, the force enough to near wind me as their arm crushed my diaphragm to stop any screaming. I wriggled and tried to kick, but they dragged me back the way I'd come, towards the alley between Will's house and the abandoned one.

"It's okay Kathryn, I have you, it's okay." Victor's voice was low and hot against my ear as I stopped fighting. "I'll let you go now. I needed to get us hidden."

He did as he said, releasing me, and I stumbled into the wall, gulping air, my watery eyes barely seeing him in the dark. "What are you doing?"

"Coming to get you, my girl. You didn't think we'd let them get away with this, did you?"

I blinked tears away, trying to catch myself. "I thought Seb would come to the table."

"He might have his own views on what's going on. He's not his father. I was with his father a long time."

I nodded, unsure if he could see me. Probably could, as a wolf. Especially tonight. "Victor, did you shoot Josh?"

"Yes. He got the drop on me, so I fired first."

"He said he was going to turn when he went out."

"Did he? He must have caught my scent before he did, careless of me. We need to move." Victor grabbed my arm, fingers sinking into the cardigan, and I pulled away, back to the wall now.

"I'm okay, I can walk."

"You're bleeding." He nodded to me, his hair catching the bathroom light.

"You can smell it?"

"I've always had a good nose for blood."

"Only Seb's better, yeah?"

"Yes. Kathryn, we really have to go now. The longer we're here, the higher the risk they'll find us."

"What's the plan? Are we running because Seb's not coming?"

"No, he'll be here, but you'll be gone, and the ensuring fight is no place for a human."

"Right. Right." I nodded, swallowing hard. "Why did you tell Will I didn't have any magic?"

Victor stilled, his head dropping, before he let out a short bark of a laugh. "Will told you that?"

"When he was busy trying to talk me around to joining his pack, yes."

"The underhanded whelp. I told him just to kill you."

"What?" Cold ran through my veins like I'd gone into deep water.

The sound of the gun cocking was loud, even over the echo of my breath, the shaking gasp that the cold metal brought when it pressed into the soft skin under my chin. "I told Will he should kill you, but he never responded. Now I see it was because he was trying to you over to his side instead, since your magic isn't as absent as you'd led us all to believe."

"Victor, you're scaring me."

"Good. You should be. Swanning back in here like you never left, flexing powers you've lied about for years. Daddy's little experiments stuck then, despite the mess he made of you."

I slid my hand as slowly as I could towards my hip, trying to keep eye contact despite the lingering tears. "I had to teach myself to use them. The flames kick in when I'm afraid, though, so you should be careful. Maybe lower the gun?"

"As I saw, at the wedding. I thought that idiot was lying when he said it was a blue fire at your house. I assumed you'd got him with oil, but no. You'd just been a better liar than a witch. But that doesn't matter. You'll be dead by the time Bastian arrives, and his anger will get him past his idealism. He'll take proper action, like he should, and with you dead, he can marry Annabelle."

"What the fuck?" I turned, stilling when he pressed the gun harder into the edge of my jaw, forcing my head up. I couldn't see his face anymore, eyes forced up to the sliver of sky visible between the roofs. "She's a child!"

"He'd not touch her until she's of age. There's too much decorum about him for that. He's not as much of a beast as some of us."

"I don't understand." My neck hurt, craned up with the jut of the gun underneath the bone. I didn't dare swallow, barely even blinked, as he huffed a sigh.

"With Michael gone, Rose crumbled to grief. I nearly did too. When I found her hanging in the garage, I knew I had to do something."

I finally got purchase at the pocket, screwing my eyes closed as I curled my fingers into the thick wool, inching the material up. "Rose tried to hurt herself?"

"Yes. She didn't though, I found her. I promised her I'd make things better. We had Annabelle to take care of. But when I went to speak to John, he was ridiculous. Ridiculous."

"How?" I had to keep him talking. Just enough to get the knife, long enough to bury it in his fucking thigh. It only took three minutes if you got the right part. I couldn't remember which part that was, but I'd take my best damn swing.

"I told him we should cement matters, join Bastian and Annabelle together. A promise, not an immediate wedding. You were useless, no value to the pack, and with Will growling at the edges, we had to have a show of power. A foundation to build from so we could be stronger from now on."

"He's more than twice her age. She's a little girl, Victor."

"So were you when your dad screwed you up. But no, John wouldn't listen. He kept saying we owed you. You!" The gun pressed harder, pushing into my neck, and I swallowed a whimper of pain. The metal ran along my skin the length of my neck.

"So you argued?" My fingertips finally touched metal, colder than the gun, and I tensed my entire arm as I wrapped my fingers around the handle.

"Not for long. I was always better with guns than John. When he wouldn't listen, I knew I had to take action. I was sad Bastian found him, but there was no other way. It couldn't be me. Inaction kills the pack."

"I think it was inertia that got Michael."

"You little bitch!" Victor reared back as if to hit me and I slammed myself forward, chin tucked low so I could shove myself into his chest and force the gun wide, hand swinging out to sink the knife into his leg. It landed wide of where I wanted, largely because of the impact of his fist on my face, sending my stance wide, but I felt the resistance of muscle, the tugging yield of the knife sliding through flesh.

He roared in pain; the gun falling as both hands went to his leg, and I abandoned the knife, lurching away from him to make a break for the parking space. He came after me, hands grabbing the cardigan, and before I could slide it off, he'd got his weight on my back, forcing us both down into the dirt.

"I don't need a gun to kill you, Kathryn. It's a full moon. No one will know the difference between my teeth and theirs."

"They will, Victor, they know you!" I twisted against his weight, trying to get around, trying to claw for him until he slammed my face into the dirt with one heavy fist to the back of my head. White exploded behind my eyes, the world muting for a breath while my brain bounced inside my head.

"I'll not leave enough recognisable for them to want to check." His weight changed, the pressure of his knees on either side of me shifting, inverting, and a low growl sounded close enough to dampen my nape before teeth sank in, forcing my face into the muddy tears below.

No, *no*, I would not do this. I wouldn't be torn apart like butcher meat for some angry old man. I scrambled around, throwing my shoulder desperately wide so I could claw my hand into his roiling shape, fur slick under my fingers as I tightened my grip and took a deep breath in.

"Stop!" I screwed my eyes closed, willing everything I had into the contact between us, the rough and shifting hair under my fingers. It wasn't as good as skin contact, the change was further along, but I could do this. I knew this. The beast could be tamed, even if my anger couldn't, and I would leave no chance for him to hurt me again.

I clenched my fist, reaching deep into the glowing shape of his change, and ripped my hand away.

Victor fell sideways, howling like I'd wounded him, and clawing at me while he twitched. Blood sprang up along my arm, cardigan and dress shredded, his claws sharp before they returned to fingers, and his snarls shifting into hacking coughs.

"What the fuck?" He punched at me, the blow glancing off my shoulder, and I nearly laughed.

"My gifts. 'Spinning silver and throwing fire. Calming the beast with just a word.' I'm that witch, Victor, just as my dad wished me to be. And now you're just a man."

"I should have killed him before he started fucking you up."

I recoiled from his words, rolling away towards the wall as he staggered into standing, swaying towards me.

"Victor!" A shout rang down the alley, a voice that made my chest swell like I'd seen sunlight in the dark, as Seb came barrelling down the dark pathway, his body colliding with Victor and sending them both barrelling sideways.

"Seb, there's a gun, careful!" I shouted, my whole body shaking from the stretch of my unruly magic, the chasing bite of the wolf spirit I had pulled out. It was tucked somewhere in me, the howl and pull of the wolf stretching against my energy, but this was wildness, a pure thrill, none of the fury and spite I had from Victor.

The sound of their fight broke my concentration, bringing me back to the dirt under my heels. The darkness that seethed with grunts and shouts.

"You killed Karl?" A punch punctured Seb's question, and I crawled closer, trying to see them.

"Not just Karl." Victor spat, blood and teeth, the red smearing across Seb's face. "I've been cleaning up messes for the pack since I joined with your father. You might be his pup, but you're nothing like him. I should have shot you instead."

Seb stepped away, backing into the wall as he panted, face twitching between a turn to the wolf and a human scream, his face elongating as the wolf won out. "No!"

"Yes." Victor loomed up, shouting, as he yanked the knife from his own leg and swung wildly as Seb, slicing into his chest, his arm, the blade arching higher.

"Stop!" I reached out, my fire lancing out like a hungry thing, a furious line separating Victor and Seb as I finally got to Seb's side, yanking him into me. "Seb, are you okay?"

He wrapped his arms around me, holding me tight, face melting back to himself. "You're here, of course I am."

"How fucking touching." Victor's voice came from the other side of the blue fire, a miserable, low sound. The leaping light showed him in sharp relief, looming like a spectre. "I'm sorry I'm going to have to do it this way, Seb. If she'd just died, it would be much easier. But now you'll both have to go."

"You've gone mad!" Seb spat, the fluid hissing against my fire.

"I wanted what was best for the pack. For all that we've done. And you were moon eyed over some stupid bitch who abandoned us." He brought up the same gun he'd had pushed into my neck, shaking in his burned hands. "I'll say you barrelled in, rushing to find her, and the Campbells acted to defend themselves. They had to.

Your sister will marry into them, as can Annabelle, and then we will be strong again. Back how we were."

"Victor, she's your baby. She's your little girl! What are you doing?" I hugged Seb tighter, slipping my heels off as I tried not to cry. If he really went to shoot us, I could shove Seb one way, tip me the other. The fire wouldn't hurt either of us, and two targets were harder to hit than one. We could still fight.

"She needs to be safe, and that means a powerful pack. We will never be strong if we have a leader who is fawning over some pathetic human with flashy tricks and the ability to strip the wolf out of us!" His face was turning red, lurid in the firelight, and the spark I had stole from him swirled within me as my anger rose.

"Seb, when I push you, I need you to run, okay?" I whispered.

"Stay with me, beautiful. I'll protect you." Seb turned, tucking himself around me as Victor bellowed.

CHAPTER 30

A booming shot rang out, and I screamed, my own animal howl in the face of it all, but no strike came. No impact, no slumping of Seb into me, no blood.

"Are you hit?" I looked up at Seb, who still had his arms around me, shaking his head as he looked about. A wet slap sounded as Victor hit the floor, followed by a gurling wheeze as he rolled onto his back. My fire died out.

"Seb." Will Campbell emerged from the deep shadows on the side of the abandoned house, aiming a shotgun at Victor's face and firing again. I whimpered, plastering myself against Seb's form, as Victor's whole body jolted, then went still.

"Will," Seb said.

"Your man had it in for you. You may have noticed." Will cocked the gun open, shedding shells before he added more in.

"I noticed you shooting him."

"Saved him shooting you. Kat, I believe I told you to wait inside."

"Victor shot Josh. He's around the back of a house, two paths that way." I pointed my thumb behind us, trying hard to ignore the creep of blood pouring out of where Victor laid. There was no way he survived that. He wouldn't get back up. I couldn't stop watching him.

"Ah, unfortunate. Still breathing when you found him?"

"Yes." I nodded, dragging my eyes up to meet Will's gaze.

He inclined his head in a small nod. "I'll get Irene to him. A fair exchange, in that case, I'll overlook your ignoring my instruction."

"She's not yours to instruct," Seb said.

"Not yours either. She's quite her own thing." Will winked, all those teeth on show again, and closed the gun. "We find ourselves in a spot now, Seb."

"Do we?" Seb asked.

"We do. I've killed your man." Will paused, spitting on Victor's body. "And he's shot my second. Can't say any of this was goodwill."

"Victor lied to you," I said. Both men turned to look at me. "I heard him say he'd told you to kill me."

Will laughed, sucking air through his teeth before he licked along his lower lip. "Right enough, he did. I changed my mind after your display at the wedding, though. You're much more fun alive."

"You were planning to kill her at our wedding?" The growl of the wolf was clear in Seb's voice and I set a hand on his chest, shaking my head.

"Peace, Seb. I'm still here."

"Victor's played us both, it seems. And we are both currently at a disadvantage. I betrayed your hospitality. I did attempt to steal your lovely wife, and I would do so again." Will winked at me, too smooth by half, and I missed my knife again. "However, I'm also standing here with a shotgun. So, I think we're about equal."

Seb nodded. "What do we do now, then?"

"You fuck off back to whatever mess you've left, coming here without back-up, and I'll get rid of this." Will kicked Victor's body.

"Just like that?"

"We come to the table again in a few days. A proper discussion, not the posturing bullshit we've had. And you bring Kat too. Irene will never forgive me if she can't check Kat over herself, and I like her company better than yours."

I blinked at Will, glancing around. "You're serious?"

"Yes. I've worked very hard to keep my wolf in so far tonight. I would love the excuse to tear something apart."

"We're not giving you women. No forced marriages," I said.

"I don't want a wife that hates me. I told you that already," Will said.

"Fine. Three days." Seb held his hand out, and Will shook it. I leaned down to grab the dagger, still slick with blood, and hid it back in the ruined cardigan. "We meet at our woods, may as well make use of the tent given all the effort of putting it up for tonight's been spoiled."

Will nodded. "I'll see you then. Hopefully with Josh, who I must attend to."

"Be seeing you, Will." Seb pushed us off the wall, and I leaned into him as support while we walked towards the carpark.

"Don't try anything before we meet," Will called. "And I'm keeping the gun."

"Fine." Seb waved a hand over his shoulder, shaking his head. "I don't want the fucking gun."

"Where's the car?" I asked.

"End of their driveway. Can you walk that far in bare feet?"

"I'd walk miles for you." I pressed a kiss to his cheek, pulling him closer.

~

The drive back was slow, the injury to Seb's arm meaning he had to be careful with how he handled the car. The silence was thick around us, oppressive as the heat of earlier in the evening, and I fiddled with the knife as I tried to bridge the gap I felt between us.

"Do we want to talk about what happened?" I asked in the gloom.

"He killed your father."

"Both our fathers."

"Yes." Seb nodded, eyes still on the road. "Both of our fathers."

I swallowed, the words heavy on my tongue. "He wanted you to marry Annabelle."

Seb gagged, shaking his head. "She's a child. She's just started to run with us. It's madness."

"He said Rose tried to kill herself after Michael died. I think… I think he went off the rails in his grief."

Seb glanced over, letting go of the gear stick to catch my hand. "I'd agree."

"They shouldn't be punished for that. Rose and Annabelle, I mean."

Seb nodded. "We'll look after them. We won't send them away."

"They might want to leave." We had, my mother and me. I don't think my mother knew Victor had been responsible for my father's death. Her rage was for the pack, but we'd still left. I could see it all about to happen again, a scared woman with a dead husband, a daughter she feared for. They deserved better than that life of fear and pain.

"I hope not. Victor died in service to the pack, in a certain way. We'll give her everything we'd give anyone else," Seb said.

"What will we tell them happened?"

Seb sighed, shaking his head. "No. He shot Josh. We can all agree on that. Will may defend his men the same way we can. That's the most neutral we can present it. The truth won't help Rose or Annabelle. There are too many secrets that should have stayed dead. Burying Victor under them brings nothing good."

"Alright."

We were silent for a few more minutes, Seb licking his lips before he spoke again. "And what about you?"

"What do you mean?"

"I saw what you did to him. When he was changing. I was part way through changing myself to get him off you."

"Oh." I smiled, too tired and too strung out from fear to do much else. No tears left. "My father's gifts to me. That's the worst bit of what he did, when he was making me better, changing my magic to be more useful. I'm like red riding hood without the axeman. I tell the big bad wolf to roll over."

"Is it permanent, forcing someone to change?"

"Not always. I can push the wolf back, or I can rip it out. Never done the latter before tonight. I can still feel it, in here." I tapped my chest, above the cuts from that first attack, not even painful anymore. It felt right that the mark of him was lurking below the marks he had caused, even indirectly.

"The wolf?"

"Yeah. A tug to the moon."

"Okay." He squeezed by hand again, nodding to me. "That's okay, beautiful. It's not a proper bite, so I don't think you'll turn. And even if you do, you're still you. No one in the pack will be afraid of you."

"I'm afraid of me."

"Well, I'm not. You're still my wife. And when we get back, and we've told everyone what's happened, we're having a bath together. I smell the blood on you. I want to know you're okay."

I laughed at him, his serious face, the way he still fussed despite the open wound on his chest. "You're impossible."

"Just as impossible as you." He tugged my hand closer, pecking a kiss to my knuckles. "My impossible mate."

EPILOGUE

3 months later

"You ready to go?" Marie stuck her head in through the door, grinning at me. She was all in white as well, a flowing dress that showed off her bump without crowding it in, and her hair was threaded with little white and pink flowers that glowed against her.

"Just about." I was in white flats this time, screw the heels, and this dress was a long-sleeved number that hid the scars on my shoulders and arm. I had a real bouquet, though the dagger was at my thigh again, a new superstition I'd be encouraging in all the pack if I had my way.

"You look fabulous. Even better than last time, if I say so myself." She winked, walking into the room to pull me into a hug. "I can't believe we're doing this."

"Given how the last one went, I'm not doing anything alone." I hugged her back, bubbling with happiness that I could see her smile so freely.

"No danger there. You're with us." She pulled back, blinking away tears, and threaded our arms together. "Let's go."

We emerged from her house to find a waiting car, pulled up with the doors open for us to get in, and Gillian already sat waiting, carrying Marie's bouquet. If she was teary-eyed, we pretended not to see it, chattering about the music choices and timings and how we hoped the sunshine would last even in the autumn uncertainty.

Once we arrived at the hall, Gillian exited the car first, opening the doors for us and giving Marie her flowers. She pulled us both into a quick hug, body pressed into mine so she didn't bump Marie's bump.

"You both look wonderful. They're both so lucky." She nodded, wiping her face quickly, then turned and walked in ahead of us. That started the music off and I nudged Marie's bare shoulder with mine.

"Let's give them a show." I winked at her.

"Hell yes."

We entered the hall side by side, equals in our dresses and our stances, both near gasping to see Seb and Daniel waiting for us at the far end of the aisle. Irene stood between them, in a vibrant pink skirt suit that made everything else glow by sheer radiation, and she smiled like the wolf she wasn't when she spotted the two of us.

Marie and I walked slowly towards the men, nodding greetings and smiles to those who had gathered for us again, and new ones too – Mrs Wilson, in a beautiful green dress, the remaining members of the Campbells who had hidden rather than risk the expected violence last time. I even nodded at Will, who inclined his head at me though Josh kept his eyes strictly forward. I didn't know if he'd ever forgive me for that morning in the woods, but I hadn't stolen his wild side, so there was no harm, really. By my measure, at least.

Once we were together with our beaus, Irene opened the ceremony, leading us through the same undertakings to the moon as Victor had months ago. There was less fear in her words, less condemnation, and while I looked at Seb, all I could think of was how much more I believed them now. We knew we would uplift each other. We knew we would love each other. And we knew we'd kill for each other, though the shotgun had eventually returned to us during the negotiations.

"You may now, both, kiss your bride."

Seb and I stepped closer, and Daniel stepped neatly around to Marie's side, both of us kissing to a whooping applause from our friends and family.

"Much better the second time around," I whispered to Seb as we parted.

"I concur." He pecked little kisses to my lips, his grin wide and handsome. "Maybe we should do it a third time, to be sure?"

"I wore the dagger, you know. I make no promises about not using it on you just because it was a gift."

He chuckled, twisting to lean me into a dip. I shrieked with laughter and kissed me again. When we came back up, he smiled at me, wrinkling his nose with such affection I could have melted. "I love you, you impossible woman."

"I love you too."

"Enough kisses. Let's get to the party," Daniel said, pointing to the doors.

"Yeah." Marie slid in beside me, joining our arms and then grabbing Daniel's too, so we were a little line of four. "Let's knock 'em dead."

Milton Keynes UK
Ingram Content Group UK Ltd.
UKHW022124291124
451915UK00010B/519

9 781915 700056